MAJOR
LEAGUE
MURDER

Also by Michael R. Geller

Heroes Also Die (St. Martin's Press)
Thoroughbreds
Disco Death Beat
Dead Last
Man Who Needed Action
Mayhem on the Coney Beat
Red Hot and Dangerous
A Corpse for a Candidate

MAJOR LEAGUE MURDER

MICHAEL GELLER

A THOMAS · DUNNE BOOK

ST. MARTIN'S PRESS
NEW YORK

Design by Holly Block

Library of Congress Cataloging-in-Publication Data

Geller, Michael R.
    Major league murder.

    "A Thomas Dunne book."
    I. Title.
PS3557.E3793M35   1988   813'.54   88-11658
ISBN 0-312-02247-6

First Edition

10 9 8 7 6 5 4 3 2 1

Dedicated to Merili . . . with love

I would like to acknowledge my friend and literary agent Mr. Dominick Abel, whose encouragement and sage advice are most appreciated . . .

. . . and Pearl, who endeavors always to make me look good.

Fingers on the Seams

· · · · · · · · · · · · · · · · · ·

Tenement courts were made for teeming children.
Playing Spalding balls in polo shirts
When summer days were counted
In popping flies, curving off the bricky ledge;
Caught like wishful dreaming of yourself
In grandstand plays,
Roaring for Yankee heroes
Blasting chorus crowds who yelled out of window radios,
Not far from where you lived.

Careful,
Not to pitch too high, or
Risk the broken window error of
The woman who you knew was never well, like
The balking umpire masked behind her curtain,
Could strike you out with boiling water
She threatened with.
Like the steamy fights your favorite player had,
When mostly safe,
But always out
Running for the plate;
On a throw
Too high and wild for you
To make it safely home.

—Kenneth Siegelman
Used here with the permission of the author.

Capaldo's was on Baxter Street, smack on the unofficial border between Chinatown and Little Italy. I walked up the short flight of stairs and stepped into a warm room with three of the dozen tables taken by customers. I waved off the coat-check girl and tried to catch the eye of Frankie Capaldo as he flitted from a back table to the bar.

There was nothing special about Capaldo's place, except for the food. Unfortunately, food was a minor consideration for the yuppie crowd who wanted potted plants and schmaltzy wine lists. Capaldo's wouldn't change. If you wanted to film a movie and catch the atmosphere of the fifties, Frankie's place was perfect.

The tin ceiling was a rust-colored shade that blended in with the redwood paneling on the walls. Each table had its own white linen cloth, real glasses, and one real flower in a vase. Up behind the bar, in a place of honor next to the liquor license, was the obligatory picture of Frank Capaldo shaking hands with Frank Sinatra. Any first-class Italian restaurant had to have Old Blue Eyes' picture somewhere on the premises. If they tried to get by with a Jerry Vale or a Dean Martin, you knew they were in deep trouble.

Frank pulled a bottle of vino from the shelf and turned to see me. I watched as the professional smile expanded into a wide open grin of recognition. "Jeesus, Slots!" He stuck out his hand. "Oh, hey, it's damn good to see you."

"Good to see you too, Frankie. How are things going?"

He shrugged. "I seen better times, but I ain't complainin'. I got Frank, Jr., in Columbia, and Gary is starting Fordham. Wendy's seein' a guy who treats her good, and Annette's healthy, so what do I have to complain about? Right, Slots?"

"Sounds good to me."

"You want something to drink or—"

"No, I'm fine. Father Quinn come in yet? He called, and asked me to rush over. He wouldn't tell me what's up."

"Yeah. He's waitin' for you in the back. You go ahead in, I'll catch you later."

He balanced the bottle of red and two glasses on a tray and threaded his way between the closely spaced tables.

There was a plain gray painted door opposite the restrooms. It had the word PRIVATE written on it. I tapped to be polite, and the familiar deep, resonant voice told me to come in.

It was a square room with no windows, painted white to ease the feelings of claustrophobia. In one corner was an old desk and the restaurant's books waiting for their monthly visit from Gary, Capaldo's son, who hoped to be a CPA some day.

Father Harry Quinn was sitting at the round card table that stood in the center of the room. He was in the process of counting piles of tens and twenties and writing the figures in a blue ledger book. I remembered that today was Tuesday, the day Quinn and his customers settled up after the weekend action and the Monday-night football game.

In addition to his duties as the priest of The Sacred Lady Church, Father Quinn was a very successful bookmaker.

"Give me a second, Slots, and I'll be with you. Have a seat while I add this up."

He was over seventy now, still a handsome man by anyone's standards. His hair and beard were snow-white over a ruddy-complexioned face, his nose and mouth surprisingly delicate. The eyes still had the cool sharpness. They peered over half-sized gold wire glasses that Father Quinn balanced toward the peak of his nose.

It had been Father Quinn who had told a very nervous Bridget Kelly that she wouldn't be facing an eternity in Hell if she married her sweetheart, one Jacob Resnick, the cantor of the Beth Zion Synagogue. A year later it was Father Quinn, along with Rabbi Heller, who officiated at the ceremonies in their respective houses of worship over the birth of Mickey Resnick, who'd later be pinned with the unlikely moniker of Slots.

Even if he hadn't been wearing the reversed collar and black dickey, it would have been hard to picture Harry Quinn as anything but a priest. There was an air of quiet assurance about him. He was the kind of man people instinctively trusted.

I had met two other people who had Quinn's qualities, and both of them had been on the other side of the law. Paul Le Blanc had swindled God knows how many women out of their money. By his count, he had been married fifty-eight times, never bothering to divorce any of the previous Mrs. Le Blancs. Even Paul admitted that his estimate of nuptials might be a bit low. It didn't matter, because not one of the thirty or so women whom we were able to track down would press charges against Le Blanc after looking at his sad eyes.

The other con man was a fellow by the name of Murray, who without benefit of even a high school education took nine CEOs of the largest corporations in the United States down a path where they emptied their wallets into Murray's Swiss bank account to the tune of $34 million. No one would have hesitated to press charges against Murray, if they could get to him. He was safely ensconced in Brazil, a guest of the government, spending a good deal of his gains securing his own palace on a tract of rich land outside the capital.

Luckily for the New York City Police Department, Father Quinn's only shady activity was his bookmaking operation. It had begun more than thirty years ago.

The Father was visiting one of his flock who was recuperating from an accident when he smelled something burning in one of the neighboring Hell's Kitchen tenements. He spotted the plume of black smoke coming out of a third-floor window and dashed across the street. The tenement had become a blazing inferno by the time he reached it, but when Father Quinn was told there was a child trapped on the second floor, he wrapped his coat over his head and plunged into the building.

After what seemed an eternity to the onlookers, Father Quinn emerged, blackened with soot, burned over twenty percent of his body. But in his protective arms he held an infant boy who had miraculously survived the flames.

Father Quinn spent three weeks in the hospital recovering from the burns. One day when he woke from a fitful sleep, he peered into the eyes of an old man.

"My name is Salvatore Trocano. The boy you saved was my grandchild, Antonio. I am eternally grateful to you. Anything that you wish . . . anything that is in my power to give you . . . you just got to ask me. You understand?"

4

Father Quinn had heard of Don Trocano. You couldn't live in New York and not know the Boss of Bosses.

"You don't have to talk now," he told the priest. "You come and see me when you're better. I won't forget what you did. You just tell me what you want." He nodded solemnly and walked away.

It had happened so quickly and so unexpectedly that Father Quinn wondered if he had been dreaming. But he did go to see Sal Trocano.

The church needed money—badly—and he asked the Don for a contribution. It was Trocano who came up with the idea for Father Quinn to get a territory.

"What you lookin' at me like that for, Father? I know the people in your church. When the collection box comes around they put their heads in their necks like they was turtles trying to get into their shells. Then they go see Little Louie, or Sonny the Barber, and hand them one, two, three dollars for the numbers or to bet on the Yanks. So, what you think? You worried that it's against the law? You gonna run bingo games in your church one day . . . and that ain't gamblin'? The government lets people bet at racetracks . . . and that ain't gamblin'? You ever been to Vegas, Father? You think that ain't gamblin'?

"No donation. I give you a territory. That way you got the money coming in all the time. Don't worry, I take care of the people on the street. Instead of them giving the money to me, they give it to you. What you say? We got a deal?"

It had started that way thirty years ago. Four different dons had ruled over the Mafia during the ensuing years, and each had respected the agreement that Trocano had made with Father Quinn. Even the police respected the bookie priest who never took a penny for himself but used the proceeds of his operation for the people of his parish.

5

Father Quinn closed the ledger book and looked up. "You don't look well, Slots. Are you feeling all right?"

"I can't shake a cold," I told him. "I've been coughing my lungs up every morning."

"Better get to a doctor, Slots. Those lingering colds could turn nasty."

"Sure, Father. I'll see a doctor right after your wedding."

Father Quinn made a tent with his fingers and stared down at them. "Sorry, Slots, I forgot."

It wasn't much of a story. Ten years ago when I wasn't feeling well, I went to a doctor who mixed up the test results and told me I had only a few months to live. That was the sort of thing that might sour a guy against the medical profession. After three days and nights of trying to get drunk but not succeeding very well, the doc called to let me know about the mistake. I went back to the quack and stuck my .38 between his eyes. It took every bit of my self-control not to pull the trigger. I walked out of his office with a whole different slant about life.

I probably took a lot of chances and I also drew my share of luck. I rose through the ranks of the department and made Chief of Detectives before Vargas became Commissioner. The very political Vargas didn't like my free-wheeling style, so I told him where he could shove his job.

I got myself a PI license and here I was a couple of years later. I wasn't rich, but I wasn't starving either. I lived in a brownstone on Thirty-third Street, which doubled as my office, and out of total vanity I drove a black 928 Porsche, which after a mere sixty-one more payments would be mine free and clear.

"How's Mom and Dad?" Father Quinn asked.

"They're doing good."

"In Florida now, I understand."

I nodded. "It's the law, Father. After the age of sixty, everybody must move down to Florida. They've got guys in golf carts patrolling the senior citizens' homes. When you hit sixty, they throw a Dolphins sweater over your head and shanghai you to a Florida-bound plane."

A smile curled the corners of his lips for a moment and then passed quickly, like luck at a craps table. He had something on his mind and I knew Harry Quinn well enough to know that he wasn't going to be rushed. I sat back and waited for him to crystallize his thoughts.

"You know, Slots, I was thinking that you don't see kids playing stickball anymore. I wonder why that is?"

"It's another sign of the times, Father. Mothers don't like the idea of their kids playing in the streets."

"Perhaps." He nodded. "I'm more inclined to think that it has to do with the fact that we're too busy organizing them into teams and leagues. I think some of the fun of the pick-up game would do a world of good. It teaches kids how to be leaders, and how to rely on themselves and not have to look to an adult for approval. I saw a group of kids outside today in front of the church. They had their bats and their gloves and they were just sitting there waiting for our youth leader to organize them. I told the boys he wouldn't be back for another half hour, but they still wouldn't budge to have a catch or practice their hitting."

"Not like our bunch."

"Lord, no! I can still see you and Tom Ryan and Paul Viggiano dodging cars and smacking those pink balls . . ."

"Spaldeens, we used to call them."

The memories drifted back to hot Saturday mornings, dousing ourselves with the spray of an open fire hydrant and slamming a ball the length of a block with a broom handle borrowed from one of our mothers.

"I could tell even back then that you were going to be a professional ball player one day."

It seemed like another lifetime. I had graduated from

7

the sidewalks and bounced into a minor-league contract with the Tigers' organization. The team I played shortstop for was the Mobile Gamers. I had been promised a major-league shot with the team at next year's spring training, but an overzealous slide by an opposing player fractured my leg . . . and my career.

Father Quinn seemed to read my thoughts. "If you hadn't been hurt, you would have made it, Slots," he told me. "You had the swing, Slots. They can't teach that sort of thing, I'm told. Either you have it, or you don't." He mimed swinging a bat. "What was it that fellow wrote about you? 'Young Resnick has the knack of meeting the ball. No matter where we put our defenders, he finds the slots.'"

"You're talking about ancient history, Father."

This was leading up to something, but I hadn't figured out what.

Quinn nodded slowly. "I thought at the time that you had received a bad break, please pardon the pun. Who could have known that you would do so well in the Police Department? Perhaps it was meant to be this way."

"Why do I get the feeling that there's a pole being greased and I'm about to go sliding down?"

Frankie tapped on the door and stuck his head in. "The kid's here, Father."

"Bring him in, Frank."

Capaldo nodded and closed the door.

"What kid?" I asked Quinn, who suddenly went deaf and was busy arranging his ledger book.

Capaldo popped back in with a young black kid who might have been twelve or thirteen. He was wearing a Sacred Lady windbreaker over his jeans. The jacket was two sizes too big for his wiry frame.

He nodded to Father Quinn and then got that look that kids get when they're alone in a room with adults without any other kids their age . . . a sort of half hound dog and half let-me-out-of-here look.

"Arthur, this is Mr. Resnick. He's the man I told you about," Quinn said.

Arthur looked up at me with a flicker of interest. Quinn must have said something nice because the kid managed a quick nervous smile.

He was a good-looking kid, with soft brown eyes and a narrow nose. There was a cleft in his chin and a hint of a dimple in his cheeks when he smiled.

"What did Father Quinn tell you?" I asked him.

"That you're going to help my father," he said in a smoky voice that was little more than a whisper.

"I haven't had a chance to discuss the . . . uh, situation yet, Arthur. I did want Mr. Resnick to meet you, though. Why don't you take these and run along back to the church?" He handed the boy the bulky ledgers. "I'll be back soon."

The kid tucked the books under his arm without saying a word. He walked to the door and got halfway out before turning around and looking at me. "I . . . I wanna thank you. My father is innocent," he mumbled, and then he was gone.

Harry and I stared at one another, "Innocent of what?" I asked warily.

"Slots," Harry started hesitatingly. "I'm not sure how I can present this to you. You see . . ." He tapped his lips with his index finger. "The boy's name is Arthur, Art, we call him. He's a good boy and he belongs to the church. His mother, Theda, works in the office. She's a wonderful lady. She's done a great job in straightening out our files and getting out the Church Newsletter. In fact, she was responsible for designing the ad for our donation flyer. I don't know what we'd do without her."

"I'll keep her in mind if I decide to open a church," I cracked.

Harry nodded absently, not really hearing me. "About a month ago she came to me, terribly upset. She walked into my office and just about collapsed in tears. Now you have to know Theda to know that isn't at all like her. She's a very private person. She explained that the kids at school were taunting the boy about his father, you know how cruel kids can be sometimes. Well, Art took it very hard and wouldn't go back to school. Theda didn't know what to do or how to handle it. It affected the boy terribly, I'm afraid. Theda thought it would pass, but it hasn't. Art wouldn't go to school, or eat, or do anything but stay in the apartment and stare out the window. I went over to see the lad and I . . . well, I promised I would help clear his father's name if he went back to school."

"And I'm supposed to make the promise good."

Quinn nodded.

"What if the guy is guilty?" I asked.

"Then that's what we'll have to tell Art. You see, it's not exactly a police matter, although it is a scandal, and it might be life or death for the boy."

I was trying to figure out why Quinn looked so uncomfortable. If it wasn't about a crime, why the big buildup?

"The family hasn't much money, so I'll provide for your fee." Harry stared down at the table.

"Harry! We're not trying to prove that Hitler is still alive or something like that?"

"No, no. Of course not."

"Good. For a second I was worried."

"His father is Jeff Davis."

Harry waited for my reaction. The pregnant pause drifted into labor and was well on its way to the teething stage before I could find my voice. "I'll take the Hitler case," I said somberly.

"I'll double your fee," Quinn countered.

I shook my head. "You don't have enough money for me to get involved with Davis." I stood up. "Get someone else, Harry."

"I don't know anybody else."

"Thumb through the Yellow Pages and stop at 'Investigations, Private.'"

"When I make a promise, I try to keep it. You're the best there is, Slots. If you don't take the case, Davis can't be cleared, and there's no telling what will become of the boy."

"Sorry, Harry. The answer's still no."

Quinn sighed and pushed himself back in his chair. "I could make it personal, Slots. I could tell you that I need you to do it as a personal favor to me. You don't have to say anything; I know that if I put it on that basis, you'd never refuse me."

Father Quinn was right. Like any good bookmaker, he knew what markers were out there for collection on a rainy day.

"I won't do that, though, Slots. I know that Jeff Davis broke your jaw with a fastball and never had the human decency to say he was sorry."

"He made a point of saying he'd do it again the next time I got a hit off him," I said bitterly.

Quinn thought about that. "I know how you feel about him. I hear the man has a knack for making enemies out of everybody. He hasn't a friend in the world."

"To know him is to loathe him."

"Do me a different favor then. Don't say no to me until you've spoken to Theda."

He wrote something down on a piece of paper and handed it to me. "That's her address. She lives in the Smith Houses. Talk to her and then make up your mind. I would be grateful to you, Slots," Harry said.

I read the address and pocketed it. Father Quinn wasn't the easiest man in the world to say no to. He had spent his life doing for others, never asking a thing for himself. There wasn't a person of any faith or color in his parish who hadn't been touched in some way by Father Quinn's works of kindness.

"This means a lot to you, doesn't it, Father?"

"They're fine people, Slots. I see something in that boy. There's a quality there that just has to be tapped. I think he's at a crossroads right now and the wrong kind of influence will push him down a path that will destroy him."

"What kind of wrong influence?"

"Talk to Theda," he said.

"All right. I'll talk to her, but I won't promise anything else."

"Agreed," Quinn said, sticking out his hand. "She'll be home tonight. I told her to expect you."

2

· · · · · · · · · · · · · · · · · ·

The level of talent between a major-league baseball player and a minor-leaguer in the Double-A or Triple-A leagues is just about the same. In fact, I've seen many an entrenched minor-leaguer with more raw talent than a lot of players in the majors. The difference between the athletes comes down to a factor that is seldom thought of by the average fan, but is very well known to inside baseball people. That factor is, plain and simple—*fear.*

There is no other occupation where a human being voluntarily puts himself in a situation of having a hard projectile hurtling toward him at speeds in excess of ninety miles an hour. With instincts developed from the birth of the human species, every nerve cell demands that the body duck out of the way. But in order to be a successful hitter at the major-league level, you've got to fight your brain's orders to bail out and wait until the last possible second to decide whether to swing, check, or protect yourself.

Years ago, the Yankees had a relief ace who could throw hard. He wore glasses that were as thick as Coke bottles. His first three warm-up pitches invariably sailed over the catcher's head into the backstop. In addition to those factors, it was common knowledge that most of the time the "fireman" was pitching bombed on a couple of six-packs. It took a special kind of player to dig in against that guy. That kind of grit is what separates the average from the star, the star from the great, and the great from the Hall-of-Famer.

Jeff Davis had drawn national attention from the moment he started pitching for his high school team in Newark. In three seasons he had lost only two games, both by a score of 1–0. He had two perfect games, seven no-hitters, and fourteen shutouts to go with his high school career totals of 23–2.

He was picked in the first round of the draft by St. Louis, who paid a premium for his services. He was sent to their top farm club, the Savannah Devils, for seasoning, where he showed that in his case the "pheenom" label was appropriate. In addition to making a reputation for himself on the mound, his off-the-field exploits also gained notoriety. His teammates reported that he was a surly bastard with a chip on his shoulder the size of a two-by-four.

There was talk that Davis had a drug problem, and he was jailed on two different occasions for putting women he was with into the hospital with severe beatings. He had several brawls with his teammates and there was even talk that the manager gave the big club an ultimatum to get rid of Davis. Instead, they canned the manager.

On the mound, Davis was imposing. Propelled by a six feet five frame and two hundred and twenty pounds of muscle, his fastball exploded into his catcher's mitt with a pop that could be heard in the last seat of the bleachers. His blazing speed and pinpoint control would have been enough to make him a standout, but Davis had an intensity that bordered on the psychotic. He considered a base hit off him a personal affront. A home run would have him storming around the mound with smoke coming out of his ears. Any player who was fortunate enough to hit one knew that the next time up at the plate, Davis was going to make him pay for it.

A professional player knows that he's going to get brushed back every once in a while. A pitcher can't let a batter set up over the inside of the plate. Those four inches turn a .250 hitter into a .300 slugger.

It's a business, after all, where you constantly have to prove yourself. Too many hits off your pitching and you're demoted to a lesser league. That means less money and less chance to make the big club. A hitter has to produce or he's long gone. He has a better bat than his predecessors, better coaching, a smaller strike zone to work with. The pitcher has the brushback pitch. The unwritten rule in the minors was that you brushed a guy back, but you didn't aim for his head.

Jeff Davis ignored that rule. He was a headhunter who seemed to delight in beaning an opposing hitter. Around the Southern League he became known as Nightmare Davis because you'd have nightmares the night before you faced him.

The first time the Gamers faced the Devils, Davis was on the mound. We had all heard from the grapevine of players who had already gone against him about how tough he was, but you had to see him in person. He was awesome; striking out the side in the first inning on nine pitches.

I was on the bench with a groin pull, which gave me an opportunity to study his moves objectively. He was, I decided, the best I had seen during my career. Not only did his hummer push the radar gun to the mid-nineties, the ball had terrific movement. Our players were consistently swinging a foot under the pitch.

I was in the lineup three weeks later, when we faced the Devils at their own ballpark in Savannah. I was batting second, and leading the league in batting with a .326 average. I could power the ball if the situation called for it but I was never going to put a scare into Hank Aaron . . . or Tommy Aaron either, for that matter. My job was to get on base and set the table for the power men behind me.

I knew that Davis would just throw smoke until I proved I could hit his pitch. I watched the first two without taking the bat from my shoulder. The count was 2 and 0, with one pitch sailing high and the other a borderline strike that the ump gave me a break on. I had good speed and was a threat to steal, so I knew he was going to come right down the heart of the plate rather than nibble on the corners, risking ball three.

I made up my mind that I was going to swing over the ball to compensate for the rise. I psyched myself to get the bat head over the plate and focused on making contact. Even with the little pep talk to myself I swung late, but I felt the ball hit the sweet part of the bat. It flared over the third baseman's head and landed in left while I pulled into second.

Davis angrily got the ball back from the shortstop and glared at me. He stepped off the mound and picked up the resin bag and then slammed it down.

"C'mon Jeff, settle down," his catcher called.

"Just catch the ball and keep your mouth shut!" Davis told him nastily.

The next pitch was another fastball that our number-three hitter never even saw. He got behind two strikes and then got a morale booster as he fouled one off.

A power pitcher gets his strength and leverage from his legs. Davis had a high chorus-line-type kick as part of his motion. I took a lead off second and made a line in the dirt that I called my launching pad. If Davis let me get to that line with his foot in the air, I was going to try and steal third. Once again he took the high kick and I passed my line and went flying into third. The catcher threw, but it was no contest. I could have gone in standing up.

"Get the ball out of your damn glove!" Davis snarled at his catcher.

The kid took off his mask and was going to answer but then he thought better of it. He crouched back down behind the plate. He didn't have to say anything. Everyone in the park, including Davis, knew that I stole the base off his windup, not off the catcher's throw.

If Davis had been glaring before, he was positively wild-eyed now. He stepped off the mound to rub the ball and tucked his glove under his armpit. His jaw was set in a tight snarl as he looked at me like a prizefighter trying to stare down an opponent before the first punch.

"What's this guy's problem?" I asked the third baseman, who was standing near the bag.

"He's a fuckin' psycho," he said. "We all hate his guts."

Davis turned his back on me and looked down at our RBI man, Horace Putnam. I made my mind up after Horace took a wild swing, making the count 1 and 2. I was going to try and steal home. Davis wasn't paying any attention to me and Horace would need a butterfly net to make contact, let alone drive me in. If they nailed me at the plate, Horace would come up next inning with a brand-new ball-and-strike count.

The trick was to time Davis' high leg kick. I inched off the bag and when the big left leg started moving upward, I chugged down the line. The catcher caught the movement out of the corner of his eye. He ripped off his mask and jumped up. "He's going! He's going!" he screamed.

Davis was well into his motion and had committed himself. He tried to pitch out to the catcher's glove, but it was too much of an adjustment to make. The ball went sailing wildly over everyone's head as I barreled over the plate, knocking the catcher, who was legitimately blocking home, down on his keester.

I was mobbed in the dugout as if I had hit a game-winning home run. I had to remind the guys that it was only 1–0 in the first inning, but it was just what the club needed, getting that important first run against Davis.

Horace swung feebly and missed, further vindicating my decision.

I came up again with no one on in the third inning. "He's going to throw at you," the kid behind the plate told me out of the side of his mouth.

He was a good-looking prospect, signed out of high school. Ordinarily, when he got a chance to play, he was talkative and filled with good humor. His demeanor today, and it was true for the other Devils too, was grim silence.

"Why? Because I stole a couple of bases?"

"He thinks you showed him up."

I planted myself in the box and waited for Davis' first serve. It was on the outside corner and down around the knees. I thought it was a ball, but the ump called it a strike, maybe to even up the one he'd called in my favor back in the first.

"It'll come now," the kid told me, shielding his mouth with his glove.

If Davis was going to throw at me, he certainly wasn't tipping it off. He was all business out there, staring in for his sign, nodding in agreement, taking a deep breath, winding up and delivering.

There's a split second when a ball is thrown at your skull when it's level with your eyes. For that fraction of time there's an illusion that the ball is larger than its actual size. It changes from a baseball to softball to beachball and then it blocks out everything in your field of vision. I felt like an animal mesmerized by the headlights of an automobile. I knew my body was trying to get out of the way, but I felt as if I were in a dream, swimming against the tide, immersed in molasses, moving so slowly, so painfully slow.

"Ball!" the ump called.

I was sprawled on the ground, aware once again of the sounds on the field and the buzzing of the crowd. The ball had buzzed my cheek like an electric shaver.

I stood up and walked out of the box, dusting myself off and playing for time. My heart was trip-hammering in my chest.

"What'd I tell you?" the kid mumbled.

I stepped back in, looking very nonchalant but making sure my hands gripped the bat tightly so as not to reveal any shaking. I wanted to be anywhere else in the world other than sixty feet six inches away from Jeff Davis.

I knew the next pitch was going to be a strike and I wasn't going to swing at it. I needed the time to get myself settled, like a guy on the ropes covering to get through the round. It was a slow curve down the heart of the plate . . . strike two!

Davis was a good actor. He seemed totally content with getting the sign and concentrating on his next pitch. He gave no indication that he threw at me on purpose. I steeled myself for the next pitch and it too was high and tight. I ducked away and felt foolish when it curved right over the plate, but a shade over the letters. I was lucky the ump called it a ball.

"Look at him step into the bucket," some leatherlung yelled from behind first.

This time Davis permitted himself a slight knowing grin. He was playing with me like a cat slapping a mouse around with his paw before he pounced.

I expected another duster but I didn't want to give Davis the satisfaction of jumping out of the way of one of his slow inside sweepers. He fired and low-bridged me.

I felt the anger inside me bubble over. Davis was as big as a house, but I had a bat in my hand. I took a step toward the mound but the ump pushed me back and walked out himself.

"Hey, what kind of shit is this, fella?"

Davis stepped off the mound toward him. "What do you want from me? The guy is taking up half the plate. I ain't lettin' him take my bread and butter."

"I've had enough of this head-hunting, Davis. Someone's going to get hurt real bad."

"Hey, the last one got away."

"Just make sure they don't get away anymore."

"I don't believe this shit! The guy's hittin' like four hundred and everyone's got to protect him like he's the fuckin' Pope."

It wasn't enough for Davis to get me out. He would

have to try and finesse me to show me up as he imagined I did to him. The script called for another slow curve. I made up my mind I was going to step into this one. If I guessed wrong and he was going to throw at me, I wouldn't have a chance of getting out of the way.

I edged my knuckles down to the end of the knob and opened my legs into what I called my power stance. Davis didn't seem to notice. He was probably imagining how foolish I was going to look as he sailed one of those sweeping curves over the plate and I ducked for cover.

The pitch was letter-high and into my *wheelhouse*. I ripped it with everything I had and felt the shock of bat crunching cowhide rippling up my arms. The only sweat was whether it would hook foul as it exploded on its way to the upper deck. I stepped into my seldom-used home-run trot as soon as I saw the first-base umpire circle his hand above his head, letting everyone know it was a fair ball.

We led 2–1 going into the seventh, with the two runs I'd generated holding up. The manager of the Devils wanted to take Davis out for a pinch hitter in the bottom of the previous inning, but the big pitcher had balked. He'd grabbed a bat and hit for himself, as the manager, remembering very well what had happened to his predecessor, sat back down on the bench, avoiding the eyes of the other players on his team.

My manager, Bucky Walsh, called me over. I was scheduled to bat third in the inning.

"I'm going to pinch for you," he told me.

"What the hell for?" I asked him.

He nodded out toward Davis. "Man's a maniac, and he didn't like you getting a home run."

"So?"

"So, son, you're a valuable piece of property, and the people in the front office are going to nail my ass if I let something happen to you."

"You can't, Buck. If you take me out, it's going to look like I was afraid to face him."

"Hell, Slots, don't—"

"I can't give the bastard that satisfaction!"

"I don't give two squirts for this macho stuff," Bucky said, shaking his head.

"Buck, if I get taken out here, it's going to get around the league that I can be intimidated. They'll all want to test me and I'll be doing gopher imitations all through the South. You've got to let me hit."

Bucky thought it over. He sprayed a brown jet of tobacco juice onto the dugout floor. "I guess . . ." he said quietly. "Okay, just get ready to do a dive."

Before I got up to the plate, the umpire was on the mound talking to Davis. I couldn't hear the conversation, but from Davis' expression I knew he was being warned. I saw Davis shake his head and say, "I can't believe this."

The ump settled in behind us and Davis threw the first pitch. It was way outside.

"How's that?" he yelled to the ump in disgust.

The second pitch bounced halfway to the plate.

"Dirty bastard," the catcher whispered. "He's giving himself an alibi."

I had already figured out Davis' plan. Davis hadn't been any more than two inches off the strike zone the whole day. Now it seemed he couldn't find the plate. If I got hit with the ball, it was because he suddenly experienced a bout of wildness.

He wound up for the next pitch and as he threw it he yelled, "Watch it! It slipped."

The ball was just like the one that had scared the bejesus out of me. I snapped my head back and it whistled past my chin.

The ump had seen enough. He ripped off his mask and stormed the mound.

"It got away, I tell ya," Davis argued.

Davis' manager ran out between the umpire and his pitcher. He put his hands behind his back and used his ample belly to get in between them. He went jaw-to-jaw with the man in blue. "This game ain't for sissies.

My man got a little wild, that's all. What are you making a case out of this for?"

"I warned him; now I'm running him out," the ump said.

"Just a second here. This place is full up with people who came to see Davis pitch. They're the ones that pay all our salaries here, Frank. Don't you go and forget that."

"Hey," I called. "It was an accident. Let him pitch. Let's get on with the game."

I reached down and held the ump's mask for him.

"There, ya hear that, Frank? Even Resnick seen it was an accident."

The umpire looked at me. "Aaahh, what the hell," he said in disgust. He walked back behind the plate. "Play ball!" he said, yanking the mask out of my hand.

I didn't want Davis to be kicked out of the game. I wanted him to pitch to me. The ball was over the plate a little on the outside corner. I choked up on the bat and put a bunt down the first baseline. It was too far down the line for the first baseman and it was rolling away from the catcher. That left it up to Davis to field the ball right near the base path.

I slowed down just enough to time his bending down for the ball. My shoulder dug into him as I ran now at full speed, catching him under the ribs and spinning him 360 degrees before he tripped and sprawled face down on the ground. I stood on first base, hands on hips, and felt no remorse as the Devil's trainer had to bring him around with smelling salts.

They carried him off the field, his big arms draped over the shoulders of the manager and the trainer. As he passed me he looked up. "You're a dead man, Resnick," he wheezed. "I swear, you're a dead man!"

I gave him a big smile.

3

. . . .

After the game we both received phone calls from the president of the league. His bottom line was that whatever had happened was water under the bridge and he didn't expect any more incidents. He told me that Davis was going to be fined a thousand dollars for hitting me after being warned by the umpire. To my way of thinking, with Davis' mega-bucks bonus contract, that would have as much impact as a flea making love to an elephant.

I agreed to refrain from any inflammatory comments or actions and the president told me that Davis had also agreed to let the matter come to an end. I told the Southern League executive that I had a hard time believing that.

"Look, Slots, I'll suspend his ass if he starts in with that beanball stuff. He'll be sittin' on the bench so long they'll be pickin' splinters out of him past Thanksgiving."

It sounded good, but he hadn't seen that wild look, and he didn't have to hit against Davis in two weeks at Gamer Stadium.

The night before the game, I joined the Nightmare Davis club. I woke up, my body drenched with sweat, as I tried to get away from a pitch that was chasing me around the base paths.

I really didn't think that Davis would be stupid or crazy enough to throw at me. His club was tied for first, and although winning the league championship wouldn't put more than an extra five or six thousand dollars in each man's kick, that wasn't small change.

Even if Davis didn't care about the money himself, he owed it to the other guys on the club to give his best. If Davis got suspended for any length of time, the Savannah team could end the season and go home.

The best thing about that day was that Davis didn't keep me in suspense. His first pitch to me was a rising fastball that started somewhere around my navel and ended up striking me in the jaw. Somehow I had raised the bat in a reflex and the ball ricocheted off the handle before hitting me flush in the face. It didn't matter too much, because my jaw had to be wired and I spent six weeks sipping food through a straw.

True to his word, the league president, Conklin, fined Davis five grand and sat him down for ten games. In interviews and in private conversations, Davis never denied that he had hit me on purpose.

It went without saying that he never tried to contact me in the hospital, not that I would have had anything to say to him.

My teammates, and even several of the guys on the Savannah club, came by to see how I was doing. Their anger at Davis wasn't put on for my benefit. I sat back as they concocted elaborate plans for getting back at the big pitcher. One of the less violent had to do with bashing his skull open with a lead pipe. In the state I was in, I didn't exactly go out of my way to talk them out of it.

As it turned out, I never saw Davis again in the minors. St. Louis was having a dismal season and here was this incredible young pitcher in their farm team. Management felt that the fans needed some hope for the future. More important, by bringing up Davis to the majors, maybe some of the sportswriters would find something else to write about and get off their collective backs.

The incident with me worked in Davis' favor. According to the team's public relations department, Davis was a "fierce competitor, a fighter, a man driven by a desire to win." No one bothered to talk to his ex-teammates on the Savannah club, whose record plummeted without their star.

I followed Davis' career with more interest than most. As detestable as he was as a human being, the man could pitch. He won seven games for St. Louis that season and followed up with a twenty-game season the next.

Over the next decade he led the league on more than one occasion in strikeouts, ERAs, and shutouts. He won the Cy Young Award and was runner-up one season for the league's Most Valuable Player.

Then, out of the blue, he was traded from St. Louis to Baltimore. On paper, the trade looked like a pretty even swap. St. Louis gave up the premier pitcher of the league for a powerhouse center fielder who might be the next Willie Mays. In addition, Baltimore threw in a slick-fielding shortstop and a pretty fair relief pitcher. For people in the know, however, something smelled funny.

St. Louis needed starting pitchers. As good as Curtis Leonard might be in the future, St. Louis had no one to make up for the fifteen games, minimum, that Davis would win for them. The St. Louis management explained that Davis was getting a bit long in the tooth, and they felt his best years were behind him. They pooh-poohed the rumors that Davis and the St. Louis manager had come to blows two times during the season.

Davis responded to the trade by winning twenty-four games for Baltimore, while Curtis Leonard finished the year batting .229. It turned out that Curtis couldn't hit off-speed pitches, of which he got a steady diet in the National League.

Davis never repeated that kind of year for Baltimore. His win totals dropped to twelve and then to a dismal campaign of six wins and thirteen losses. He was traded to Texas, where he won seven games one year and just four the next. The Texas management asked him to go to the bull pen and Davis refused. He was sent down to the minor leagues and most people wrote him off.

It was a familiar refrain. A pitcher gets older and loses a few yards on his smoke and suddenly the hitters are catching up to him. In Davis' case, his ball had the same velocity, but that rising, moving action wasn't there anymore. That should have been the end of Jeff Davis, but the man insisted he would be back—and he was right.

According to the sportswriters, a pitching coach in the minors taught Davis the "slip" pitch, where the ball is thrown hard and just slips out between the middle and index fingers. The effect was to give the ball a downward rotation, and it seemed to drop just before home plate. With that trick pitch added to his repertoire, Davis bounced right back to the majors. In his first season back he won twenty games and pitched his second no-hitter. The following year he won eighteen games, losing only four, and led his Texas club into the league play-offs in New York.

That had been three years ago, and it marked another time that I crossed swords with the star player.

A couple of days before Davis and company were to play at the stadium, there had been a racial incident a couple of blocks from the ballpark. A black church had been firebombed and the worst kind of racial epithets had been written on the walls of the building.

Davis had been asked about how he felt about coming to New York, particularly in such an emotionally charged period. His reply was that it was never comfortable for any black man or woman in racist America. When asked specifically about the church incident, he said, "The police know the folks that did this thing, but since they agree with killing black people, they're not going to do anything about it."

The reporter asked if he had any proof that the police knew who the perpetrators were and Davis stated, "Hell, you got a Chief of Detectives in this town named Resnick. He's worse than Bull Connors ever was in the old days. This Resnick is the number-one racist in this town. You think he's going to do anything to protect black folks?"

It was one of those *When did you stop beating your wife* things, which are really impossible to answer. I played it very straight, denying we had any information and declining to comment on Davis' charges against me personally.

I watched as the media chased their own tails and Davis' words moved from the sports pages to the front pages to the editorial pages. Incredibly enough, a movement was started to put pressure on the Commissioner to get me to resign. The Mayor's Police Department liaison, Morris Ackerman, scheduled briefing sessions with me every day to find out how the investigation was progressing and to warn me not to speak to the press.

I knew Davis must have been getting a kick out of making me squirm, but then two things happened that changed everything around.

Number one, we caught the firebomber. He was a deranged neo-Nazi who had been in and out of mental institutions. And two, Davis got caught with a mittful of Vaseline.

From the beginning, there had been a lot of people who doubted the "slip" pitch story. In their minds, the story of the old coach showing Davis a pitch that resurrected his career was as much a myth as fire-breathing dragons or twenty-year-old virgins. They felt that the ball moved the way it did because of certain foreign substances that were "slipped" on it. By scuffing a ball, or nicking it, or placing a piece of gum, tar, wax, or something else across the seams, it would behave just like Davis' pitch. Throughout the season, much to Davis' annoyance, opposing managers and hitters would stop the game and ask the umpire to check the ball for illegal substances. No one had ever found anything until that first play-off game in New York.

A win by Texas in that first game of the play-off series would have set the stage for them to take the pennant and go to the World Series. With Davis on the hill, even the New York players admitted privately that it would take a miracle to beat the Texans.

Early in the game, the imposing pitcher overwhelmed the opposition. He struck out the side in the first, and had struck out the first batter in the second. The umpire called time and walked to the mound. He took the ball from Davis and checked it. Then he pointed to Davis' glove. The pitcher looked puzzled and handed it to the umpire.

Davis' manager ran out to the mound to find out what was going on, but got no explanation. Instead, Augie Casillo, the plate umpire, who was also the crew chief, called in all the other umpires and they had a meeting just off the first baseline. Each of the men passed around Davis' glove and inspected it.

Jeff Davis stood on the mound seemingly bewildered. Then Casillo said something to him and he exploded. He had to be restrained from attacking Casillo, who took Davis' verbal abuse for twenty seconds and then, in a wide thumbing gesture, tossed the enraged pitcher out of the game.

The papers told the full story the next day. Casillo had found the inside of Davis' glove loaded with Vaseline. He had obviously been using the substance to doctor the ball. When he was informed that the glove was going to be confiscated and sent to the league office, Davis went crazy. He insisted he didn't have Vaseline in his glove and he was being framed by the "white establishment" of baseball. He swore he'd get Casillo for what he'd done and threatened the umpire's life in front of TV and newspaper reporters.

The Commissioner of Baseball promised an investigation, but Davis refused to cooperate in any way with the "kangaroo" court. "They think they got this nigger hung out to dry," he was quoted as saying.

Texas lost the Vaseline Game, as it became known, and in its wake, the play-off. Eventually, over the off season, Jeff Davis was suspended indefinitely for conduct unbecoming to baseball. He was pictured in *Sports Illustrated* showing in gesture what the Commissioner could do with his suspension and with baseball.

Now, thanks to Father Quinn's promise to little Arthur, all I had to do was turn back the pages of history three years and clear the name of my warm and good friend, Jeff Davis.

I wondered why I couldn't seem to generate any enthusiasm for the job.

4

he Smith Houses were a collection of seventeen-
story brick apartment buildings just a couple of
blocks from my old haunts at Police Plaza. Although the buildings were low-income projects, they
were well kept, with pleasant grounds that were beginning to show the blooming face of spring.

I took an unsteady elevator ride to the fourth floor
and punched the buzzer at apartment 4E. The sound,
something between a telephone ring and a travel
alarm, got the door open about three inches on the
chain lock.

"Yes?"

I couldn't see much of the woman on the other side
of the door but what I could see seemed pleasant
enough.

"I'm Resnick. Father Quinn told me you'd be expecting me."

I heard the chain rattle and the door opened wide.

"I'm Theda," she said, extending her hand. "Please
come in."

She was a light brown-skinned woman in her thirties with very big eyes and a smile that belonged in a toothpaste commercial. Her hair was pulled straight back, which served to accentuate her high cheekbones and long neck. She wore blue jeans and a pink blouse that matched the pink doodad holding her hair in place. If I closed my eyes for a second I'd have no trouble picturing her in a tutu and ballet slippers doing pliés in *Swan Lake*.

She ushered me to a chair in the kitchen. I could see the whole layout of the place from the table. There was a moderate-sized living room with a sofa bed, a dinette, and, guessing from the bike in the doorway, Arthur's bedroom.

There were a lot of little touches that showed Theda had spent some time around colors and textures. The kitchen was done in an off-white paper with little shoots of straw and flashes of yellow. There were wicker planters hanging close to the window and a collection of wicker baskets on the far wall. I sat in a cane-back next to a table whose brown hue was captured in the light marble-colored linoleum.

The living room was done in a Spanish motif. There was an etching of Don Quixote and Sancho plodding off into the sunset opposite a wall featuring a brightly colored blanket with a Moorish design. The sofa bed picked up the colors and sported delicate mantilla-like lace along the armrests. There was no carpet, and the wood floor wasn't parqueted, but someone had stained it and polished it to a high gloss, which gave it a very finished look. It was done inexpensively yet elegantly, and I was impressed.

"You know how to put a place together," I told her.

That won me one of those toothpaste smiles.

"Decorating is my hobby. My one vice is the *Architectural Digest*. I've got a closetful of them. You can pick up some good ideas and you don't have to spend a fortune."

There was a warmth to her voice and a quality of vulnerability which, looks aside, would be attractive to most men. I had to remember that she was Davis' wife.

"It's hard for me to picture you married to Jeff Davis," I told her.

Her eyebrows shot up. "Really?" The corners of her mouth fought back a smile.

"I said something amusing?"

"I'm sorry, Mr. Resnick. I know you don't realize it, but you just paid me a big compliment. I wouldn't want to be anything like Jeff. We have nothing in common, and we were never married. My full name is Theda Andrew."

"But you do have one thing in common." I nodded toward the boy's room. "Arthur."

She thought about that, shook her head and sighed.

It was time to lay out the ground rules.

"Let me tell you from the start," I said, "that Jeff Davis is very low on my list of favorite human beings. He beats out Mengele and Ivan the Terrible, but only by a whisker."

"Father Quinn told me you felt that way."

"Good. I'm here out of courtesy to Father Quinn and I'm kind of hoping that by knowing how I detest Davis, you'll want someone else to clear the bastard. Pardon my language."

"I'm from St. Nicholas Avenue and One Hundred Twenty-fifth Street. You won't shock me, Mr. Resnick."

"Make it Slots."

"I've got a fresh pot of coffee, Slots. How do you take yours?"

She stood up and brought two mugs close to the Mr. Coffee.

"Black, no sugar."

I watched her pour. I think you can tell a lot from the way a person pours coffee into a cup. If they hold the handle of the cup with their other hand, they're conservative, guarded, and generally afraid to take a chance. Pour it one-handed and you've got spontaneity, openness, and a gambler.

Theda started out one-handed and then grabbed the handle midway. I called it a draw.

"I was going to college in Missouri and a friend talked me into seeing a baseball game. I didn't know a bunt from a hole in one, but this friend of mine knew the game and some of the players. We wound up meeting a couple of them for drinks at the hotel where they were staying. Jeff was a handsome, wealthy baseball player, and I was a little girl from Harlem. We started seeing each other and . . ." She shrugged. "It didn't work out."

"Why?"

"If he won, he was great fun to be with. When he lost, he was a monster. He would go out of his way to pick fights with everyone. He'd drink and just get crazy—and physically abusive. I still have scars . . ." Her voice trailed off.

I nodded and waited for her to continue.

She took a sip of coffee and looked out the window. "I had a lot of people tell me that I should have done something about the baby, but I've never regretted my decision."

"Jeff didn't agree?"

"Honey, he was gone the moment he heard I was pregnant! I didn't see him and I didn't see a dime from him."

"It must have been tough for you."

"I was a black single parent in a strange town without a job or any prospects of getting one—too proud to go on welfare and too ashamed to go back home. My father and mother were very religious people and it would have broken their hearts.

"Eventually, when Arthur was about a year old, I took him with me to the players' entrance of the stadium. We waited there a couple of hours until Jeff came out. When he saw me, he rushed past us. I called

3 4

out to him, 'Don't you even want to take a look at your son?' You know what he said to me?''

I had an idea but I kept it to myself.

"He said, 'That ain't my son, and I never seen you before, bitch!'"

"That sounds like his deft way with words."

"You know, Slots, as crazy as this may sound to you, until that moment I think I still loved him, but to hear him say that to me . . ." She shook her head.

"You could have taken him to court and made him assume the financial responsibilities," I told her.

"Oh, I did. It was a very long-drawn-out affair and it was one hell of a fight. He denied even knowing me. Under my lawyer's cross-examination, and the threat of perjury he finally admitted he might be Arthur's father. That's all I wanted, really. I couldn't let him just walk away pretending I never existed and that his son never existed. I made him pay for all the court fees, and that's it. I didn't want anything more to do with the man, and that included his money."

She looked at me with her chin set defiantly. "That was the last time I saw him, and good riddance."

"Arthur doesn't feel that way."

"No," she admitted. "I made mistakes in how I handled things and they're coming back to bite me now. I never told Arthur who his father was. I led him to believe his father was dead."

"He found out differently?" I prodded.

"I was at work, and he found the court papers. He was nine then, and you never saw a little boy so angry. I tried to explain to him that in my mind his father really was dead. I don't know . . . you try to do the right thing. Sometimes it just backfires. He made me tell him all about Jeff, and you should have seen him sitting there like a blotter soaking everything up. The more I talked against Jeff, the more his little chin would stick out."

She shrugged resignedly.

"He was very proud that his father was a sports celebrity. He made me buy every newspaper so he could pore through them just in case his father's name was mentioned in the sports pages. Jeff was just about out of the majors then. He was working on his comeback pitch. Artie even bought *The Sporting News* because they used to cover minor-league teams."

"Did he ever try to see Jeff?"

"Only every day." She laughed. "He'd make phone calls and he'd send letters. He'd hear that so-and-so came from a town where Jeff pitched, so he'd tell them to look up Jeff for him. But we never did hear from Jeff. The funny thing was that Arthur wasn't too disappointed. I mean, I knew he wanted to talk to his father, but when the mailman said there was no letter he would just shrug and try again."

"Maybe it's hard to miss something you never had," I said.

"That and the element of hope. You keep figuring that tomorrow will bring something good. We had one very bad time, though. When Jeff got back that last season . . . I think he was playing for Texas . . ."

I nodded.

"Well, he came into New York and all Arthur wanted was to go to the ballpark and wait for his father at the players' entrance."

"*Déjà vu.*"

"Exactly. Well, I couldn't do that. It was hard enough for me to think about seeing that man again. I came up with another idea. I knew the team was staying at the Sheraton and I took Arthur with me. I told him we wouldn't be able to go upstairs and see Jeff because then everyone would bother him and he wouldn't be able to pitch. He looked up at me and said, 'But if he knew it was me, Mommy, he'd let us see him.' He wrote this wonderful little letter, with these stick-figure pictures . . . I mean, it was so touching. Well, I wrote a note too. Mine said that if I had ever meant anything at all to him, I was begging him to do this one little thing for me. Just come down for a minute and say hello to the boy."

Theda's eyes misted. She wiped one delicately with the tip of her index finger.

"One of the team's security men stopped us on the floor where Jeff was. He told us we couldn't go any farther. I explained that Arthur was Jeff's son and that he just wanted to say hello. Y'know, they have this list, and if you're not on the list you can be the Almighty but you still aren't getting any farther.

"Jeff tugged at the guard's pants and said, 'Please let me see my daddy.' I showed him the little note that Arthur had written and the man's voice kind of choked up a little. He took both of our messages and told us to wait and he'd be right back. I know he brought the messages in to Jeff because he came back about ten minutes later with this funny look on his face. 'I'm sorry, little man,' he said to Arthur, 'your daddy's not here right now.' You could see Arthur's face just fall down.

"As we turned to leave, the man handed me the letters. 'I tried,' he whispered to me. 'If you ask me, lady, a man like that doesn't deserve a nice kid.'"

We both took time to sip our coffee. It was a comfortable silence. Downstairs a siren went through the Doppler effect and the apartment's fridge kicked into gear.

"Why is it so important to clear his name?" I wanted to know.

"This past year Arthur started junior high school. When he was in elementary school the scandal broke. I don't think he really understood what happened and the kids in his school didn't make a big deal out of it."

"And in junior high they jumped all over him."

"Exactly. Over a single summer the same nice little boys turned into vicious animals. They started calling him names like the Vaseline Kid, and Greaseball, and

Spittoon. He would come home one day after another, the knees of his pants ripped, dirt all over him, and a bloody nose or a black eye . . . all because he was defending the name of that no-good SOB who pretended he never even had a child.

"It was enough to make me think about moving away and starting all over again without anybody knowing a damn thing about us."

"Why didn't you?"

"Two reasons. It takes money, for one . . . and what Father Quinn said was true. There's always going to be someone who knows and you might as well fight here as anyplace else."

"Clearing Jeff is part of that fight then?"

"Hell, no! The happiest day of my life was seeing Mr. High and Mighty get his. It's just that Arthur has built this thing in his head that Jeff is innocent and he's obsessed with that. Taking guff from the other kids just makes him want to prove it more."

"Father Quinn mentioned something about Arthur getting into trouble."

"Yes." She dug something out of the pocket of her jeans. "I was collecting laundry and I found these tucked inside a pair of his rolled-up socks."

She opened her palm and showed me the pills in a piece of tissue. They were Seconals, red birds.

"That's a very powerful drug. Was he using or selling?"

"Neither, he was collecting."

It took me a moment to figure it out. It added up. The kid had those sad eyes, the brooding, the not wanting to go to school.

"I found out that suicide is the most common cause of death among teenagers, Slots. When I questioned him, he told me that he thought about taking a whole bunch of pills and then just going to sleep."

She covered her face with her hands and sobbed without making a sound. She wasn't looking for comforting. She had worked this out already and was just shaken for the moment. I gave her time to compose herself.

"Where did he get them?"

"Drugs are all over the place. They pushed the addicts away from the Bowery, so they set up shop around here," she said disgustedly. "I give him lunch money—and he's buying pills."

"Do you think he really was serious about it?"

"God help us, yes," she said quietly. "I'm scared to death about opening a window or leaving a knife around. I have nobody to watch him, and you can't watch a thirteen-year-old boy twenty-four hours a day.

"Father Quinn has just about saved both of our lives. If it wasn't for him, I don't . . . He's been talking to Arthur, sometimes they talk for hours. A couple of days ago, Arthur came home all excited. I mean, it was the first time in months that I saw the boy actually smile. Father Quinn told him about you and he was sure you'd show everybody that his father wasn't a dirty player."

I walked the cup to the sink and gave it a rinse.

"I don't want to do this. I don't want any part of this case, or Jeff Davis."

It came out angry.

Theda seemed to wince.

I was being pushed against a wall. The kid's fixation with his old man wasn't my concern. Quinn, Theda, the goddamn Seconals . . . I had better things to do with my time.

"I understand," Theda said, putting up a brave smile.

"No, you don't understand. I'm not sure I understand."

How could I put feelings that were gut-level into intelligent sentences?

"It has something to do with freedom, and making my own choices, and not letting anyone or anything shape my life. How do I say no to a mother who's scared to death her son's going to kill himself? Or how do I say yes and do something to help a miserable bastard like Jeff Davis?"

Theda shrugged. "The old rock and a hard place," she said sadly. "All I can tell you is that as much as I despise Jeff, I love Arthur more."

"What happens if I find out that Jeff is guilty as charged?"

"I've talked to Arthur about that."

"And?"

"He can handle it. He just wants his father to have a chance. I think he understands the odds."

"That's a tough nut for a thirteen-year-old," I told her. "I'll have to talk to him before I make a commitment."

"All right," she said. "I think that's a good idea. He's probably around the back in the schoolyard."

I said good-bye and walked to the door. As I reached for the knob, I turned. "You better give me the last address you have for Davis—just in case."

Arthur wasn't with the kids in the park. I walked around eyeing everyone five feet tall or less. He wasn't playing basketball in the neighboring schoolyard either.

I walked around another ten minutes and then headed for my car. I had parked it just a couple of feet overlapping the yellow of a bus stop. I hoped that my old Police Department permit might finesse me out of a ticket. I'd be okay as long as the Traffic Enforcement people didn't look too closely at the expired date.

What were the chances that a Brown Coat would pass up a chance to ticket a jet-black Porsche sporting a PD visor? I knew the answer to that one, but I was surprised on two counts. First, no ticket. Second, there was Arthur leaning against the hood.

"Hi. How are you?"

"Okay," he mumbled.

"How did you know this was my car?"

He pointed to the vanity license plate with SLOTS written out in the gold-colored frame.

"Let's not forget who the detective is around here," I kidded.

He nodded, not sure if I was being serious or not.

The kid had Theda's big eyes. His hair was cropped close to his head, and the rest of him was all gangly arms and legs. He would fill out and stretch and be a giant like his father. I wouldn't want to be in the shoes of the school wise guys if Arthur had a good memory.

"You hungry?" I asked him.

He shrugged.

"Well, how about keeping me company while I get something?"

I could tell he liked the idea by the way he scrambled into the Porsche. I found a clean-looking diner three blocks north, and a parking lot that gave you a discount if you got your ticket stamped by the diner's cashier.

A heavyset waitress took my omelet order and Arthur broke down after a minute and asked for the burger deluxe.

"How's the food here?" I asked him, and got the now familiar shrug.

I always lacked the patience it took to be good with kids. I talked to Arthur about the weather, school, cars, even which recording group was his favorite. I got a couple of shrugs, an "Uh-huh," an "I don't know" and a name like "Moongus Foopoo," which I wasn't sure was a man or a woman or a group. Arthur wasn't making it easy.

I was about to sink my pearly whites into my eggs when Arthur broke his silence.

"You hit against my dad, didn't you? Father Quinn said you played in the minors against him."

"Father Quinn's right," I said, putting down my fork.

"Did you ever get a hit off him?"

"Homered," I told him.

You could see the kid's face cloud up.

"But that was because he gave me a curve and let me hit it."

The sun came out again.

"He was the greatest, wasn't he?"

I didn't have to lie. "He was the best pitcher I ever saw, Arthur. His fastball was unhittable, and he had great control."

Arthur positively beamed.

"Did you play in the majors, too?"

"Nope. I got hurt and had to leave baseball."

"Could you tell me more about my dad?"

"Why don't you tell me about him."

"Okay."

He rattled off all the statistics—the perfect games, the no-hitters, his lifetime earned-run percentage, his strikeouts, walks, shutouts. He went on for a good three or four minutes.

"You sure know your stuff," I said.

"You know why? 'Cause I want to be just like him."

He lifted his shirt and showed me the baseball jersey underneath. He was wearing number 13, Jeff's number.

"You pitch?"

"For two teams, school and my church."

"Any good?"

"Yeah. I mean okay."

"I'll bet you're very good."

He shrugged again, but this time a smile went with it.

"You're going to help my father, aren't you?" he asked.

"Why is it so important to you?"

"Because he didn't do it. I know he didn't."

"How do you know?"

"He tole me."

"I thought your mom said you hadn't spoken to him."

"He tole me when he was on TV. He said he was innocent and he was framed."

"Why do you think anyone would want to do that to him?"

"I don't know."

"How would you feel if I went out and looked into the case and found out that your dad really did load up the ball?"

"That can't be. He said he didn't."

"Come on, Arthur. People make up stories; even your dad could make up stories."

He took a big bite out of his burger and chewed it slowly.

"I think I know how important your dad is to you, but this isn't a fairy tale. It may not come out with a happy ending."

He looked up at me. "I know that . . . I really do. I just think my father should have a chance. If he did do what they said, at least I'll know it for sure."

"And then what? Get more Seconals?"

He was surprised I knew about that. He looked down at his plate and talked softly. "I'll never do that again. Father Quinn explained it to me about how selfish I was, not thinking of my mother and the other people who love me. I promised I would never do anything like that again."

"I hope not, Arthur. No matter what your dad did or didn't do, nobody could ever call him a quitter. If you killed yourself, that's what you'd be—a quitter."

"Please say you'll help my dad," he asked.

"Arthur, what do you think is going to happen, even if I do prove him innocent? The kids who are bullies are still going to be bullies. He can't come back to baseball. They're still going to call you names. What's going to change?"

"Nothing, I guess . . . but maybe . . ."

"Maybe what?"

"I can't tell you."

I sighed and finished my meal. The kid wolfed down the rest of his deluxe and had the rare good manners actually to thank me. In spite of my reservations about kids, I liked Arthur.

We drove back to his apartment building. On the way, I fooled with the radio while Arthur stared out of the window. We made a little small talk and then I pulled up in front of his door.

"Well, this is it," I said.

He grabbed the handle of the door but didn't pull it open. Instead he turned to me. "If I tell you what might change, do you promise not to laugh, or say anything?"

"Yeah."

He wrestled with himself for a moment. "Sometimes I think that if I help my father and clear his name, he might love me and come to see me."

He opened the door and ran into the building, not looking back.

5

· · · · · · · · · · · · · · · · · ·

I drove north on the FDR, mentally kicking myself for being such a soft-hearted sap. The address Theda had given me was over on the Upper West Side, so I cut across on Ninety-sixth Street and pulled into a spot off Broadway.

Davis was living in a once elegant building that had seen better days. A new canopy in the front, two weeks of sandblasting the tired bricks, and new windows would have doubled the property value.

I gave the doorman Davis' name and he rang the bell.

"I don't think he's home," he told me while we both waited. "Friend of his?" he asked.

"I don't think he's got any friends," I told the old gent.

"You got that right," he said, nodding. "Nah, he's not home."

"Okay, thanks anyway."

I was halfway out the door when he came after me. "Around the corner there's this bar called Smokey's. He usually spends his time there."

I peeled off a buck and got a spiffy touch of the cap for a thanks.

Smokey's was a hole-in-the-wall with a red neon sign that flashed SMOKEY'S TAVERN against a dirty window. True to its name, the place had a pungent cloud of cigarette and cigar smoke, mixed with the sweet, sticky scent of booze.

It took me a moment to get my eyes accustomed to the darkness. There was the usual mahogany bar, with four flies sitting shoulder to shoulder balancing cigarettes and nursing beers. Toward the back there were booths, red Naugahyde platform benches with tufts of slush-colored foam peeking through ripped seams.

Davis had his back to me. I knew it was Davis because of his broad shoulders and his polished black skull. It was like the Washington Monument balancing a bowling ball.

Facing me opposite Davis was a bleached blond harpy with a shrill laugh not unlike fingernails on a blackboard. Her garish lipstick and eye shadow would have earned her a job with Barnum & Bailey. She squinted and cocked her head as I walked toward her. She was too vain for glasses.

"Who's this?" she asked as I stood next to the booth.

Davis looked up at me. He hadn't changed much. He still had the moon face, squashed nose. A drooping mustache curled down over his full lips. His eyes were heavy-lidded, as if he had just blown some weed or polished off a few inches from the bottle of Johnny Walker Black he had in front of him. If he recognized me, he didn't give it away.

"Whatever you're sellin', take it somewhere else," he rumbled.

"I'd like to talk to you. It won't take too long and it might be important to you."

"Yeah."

He stared at me and I returned the look.

"We were in the middle of a conversation, mister," Blondie squealed. "You got a lot of nerve."

4 6

I fished out a ten and handed it to her. "Get yourself a bottle and powder your nose. I'll be gone in a few minutes."

She looked over at Davis, who nodded.

"I'll see you later, Dee," she purred.

She slid out of the booth, adjusted her skintight skirt and walked back to the bar.

I took her place across from Davis. "Remember me?"

"I don't forget white motherfucker assholes, so why would I forget you, Resnick?"

"Nice to see you too, Davis. Now that we got the pleasantries out of the way, I'll tell you why I'm here."

"I don't give a shit. I let you sit down because I was tired of the broad slobbering all over me. Why don't you take a walk?"

"There's someone who believes you didn't load up the ball three years ago. He's hired me to clear your good name."

He ignored me and poured four fingers of Scotch into his glass.

"Before I get myself too far involved and I take my client's money, I'd like to know what really happened. If you were bullshittin' everybody about being innocent, you'd be saving us all a lot of time by telling the truth."

He tossed the Scotch down his throat with one swallow and poured another glass.

"You've come down a few pegs, haven't you, Slots? I heard you were a keyhole peeper now." He wiped his mouth with his sleeve.

"You ain't exactly the crown prince of rock 'n' roll yourself," I told him.

"I got nothin' to say to you, white bread. Take a walk!"

"Kid by the name of Arthur believes in you. It's nice to see a kid that loves his old man. A lot of punks in school are giving him a tough time. They call him names and he's been in a few fights. He won't let anybody say anything against you. I'd like to help him out, but I need you to tell me you're clear, otherwise it's just going to be worse for the boy."

He leaned close to me. "I told you to beat it. Get out of my face!" He reached out and grabbed my shirt in a big paw.

"Got a problem, bro?"

Two men appeared at the booth looking down at us. Davis let go of my shirt.

They were black men in their twenties. One was broad, over six feet, and bulging out of a muscle T-shirt. The other was the same height, bone-slim, with a black fedora and sunglasses. He was also pointing a gun at the bridge of my nose.

"Just stay calm, bro. Let's see what we got here."

He reached into my jacket and pulled out my .38.

"Lookee here! You said you were lookin' for a nice gun, Mitts. Look what the man brought for you."

Mitts grunted and stuck the gun in his waistband.

"Get this piece of shit out of here," Davis said, "and if his leg should get broken along the way, I won't shed no tears."

"Gotcha! C'mon, bro, you heard what my main man said."

I didn't move. "You're out of your league here, dip-shit. Take your Bogart patter back to the mirror and practice up a little more."

"Hey, Mitts, this man ain't movin' hisself. See if you can help him up."

The big guy's hand settled on my left shoulder. He was nicknamed Mitts for a good reason. He could play first base without a glove. He squeezed, and I got up. It was either that or a broken shoulder. The son of a bitch was like a vise.

"Follow me, bro. We'll go out the back to the alley, where we'll have more privacy."

"Be right back," I told Davis.

"Not in this life," he said.

They marched me out, one on either side of me.

Slim's gun was burrowing into my rib cage and Mitts had his left hand around the back of my neck as if I were wearing a choker. I had no doubt that he could break it by giving a half squeeze.

Slim opened the fire door and we were in a courtyard that would look like dusk no matter how bright the sun. There were two garbage cans, three brick walls, and a long alleyway that led out to the street.

"Do his right leg," Slim said, drawling it out.

I waited for the big man's grip to leave my neck. I had learned to fight at a young age. You didn't survive being half Jewish and half Irish in Hell's Kitchen if you didn't know how to take care of yourself. As kids, we never bothered with judo, karate, kung fu, or any other formal martial arts. We were strictly New York City street fighters. It wasn't pretty, but it got the job done.

Slim had the gun, so he was first. His mistake was keeping the gun too tightly pressed to me. I gave a half turn and the gun twisted to the side. I reached down and pressed it against my hip so Slim couldn't draw it back and shoot. It was pointing sideways down the alley. In the same motion, I crouched down and brought up an uppercut squarely to the thin man's groin.

He made a sound between a gasp and a dry heave and reflexively squeezed off a shot that harmlessly went into the ground. I body-checked him hard into the brick wall, sensing the roundhouse from Mitts behind me that went whizzing past my ear. I made a grab for Slim's gun but it dropped from his hand and fell a few feet away. He crunched into the wall and sank slowly to the ground.

Mitts cursed and reached out to grab me. He was slow and muscle-bound, and I was able to dodge him. He telegraphed his right, so I slipped in underneath and caught him on the chin with a hard left hook. I might as well have punched a battleship. He didn't even blink. He snatched at me, trying to get a hand on any part of my body. I picked up the lid of a garbage can and clanged it off his head like the cymbals in the "1812 Overture." The guy didn't notice. He ripped the cover from me and hurled it like a Frisbee.

There was only one spot that wasn't protected, and I knew I would have to get close to him. He charged, and I waited. He reached for me and I sliced upward with the side of my hand, catching him flush in the throat. His tongue stuck out and his eyes bugged. He wheezed for breath and clutched at his windpipe.

I stepped in and swung from my heels. It was an uppercut that would have lifted a normal man off his feet. Mitts's head bounced back six inches. He was still clutching at his throat and making gurgling sounds. I grabbed him in a headlock and rammed him into the wall. It was either him or the building, and this time the building stayed up as Mitts collapsed next to Slim.

I made sure the big guy was out cold before I reclaimed my gun from his waistband and walked back into the bar. Davis hadn't moved from his spot. It was a still life of *Man Staring at Whiskey Glass*. I broke the tableau by tossing my card down in front of his face.

"If you get bored feeling sorry for yourself, give me a call. If you lose the card, I'm in the book."

He looked past me for his friends.

"They're in the back taking a nap," I told him.

I headed back downtown wondering how much of my time, and Father Quinn's money, I should invest in this case. Jeff Davis wasn't making it easy to prove himself innocent. Of course, I didn't have to find him innocent. All I had to do was get the facts and come to a conclusion one way or another. That would mean looking at the tapes of the game, interviewing some of the principal witnesses, and then tying everything up in a neat little package.

My brownstone office fell under the shadow of two giant condos, which stood like sentries on the corner of Thirty-third Street. The bottom floor was mine, well furnished, slick and modern.

The office and the Porsche ate up a good piece of my Police Department pension check, but I stretched things out by using the office as an apartment. The sofa pulled out to a convertible bed and the small kitchen off the main room was adequate for my far from gourmet tastes.

I punched in the "play" button on the answering machine and went through two or three hangups before a human voice came on. It was a salesman making a pitch for life insurance. If I would call him with my birth date, he could save me a lot of money, particularly if I were a nonsmoker.

I rewound the tape and settled into the chair behind my desk. I had been a nonsmoker now for a number of years. I'd dropped the weeds when I found myself waking up at three in the morning in the clutches of a nicotine fit, with not a butt in the house. I had put on my bathrobe, thrown a raincoat over that, and walked three blocks to a twenty-four-hour grocery in a mini-hurricane. Later, standing soaking wet in a puddle up to my ankles, I vowed to enjoy the twenty smokes because there wouldn't be any more.

I stared at the phone and pondered my next move. There were some connections I still had from my playing days.

I had an acquaintance in the Baseball Commissioner's office. His name was Dan Williams and he had been a third-string catcher on the Gamers when I played for them. Ducky, as we called him because of his waddling walk, had ended his career as a player in the minors, had coached, and then managed. I had read a couple of years ago that he had been tapped by the Commissioner to represent the minor leagues. They gave him the title Director of Minor League Affairs. His job was to help the floundering clubs in the minors get TV or cable contracts to keep the franchises going. He did most of his work entertaining beer barons and convincing them to purchase advertising time and to fill the billboards in the outfield with their messages.

I thumbed through my book for his number and got a throaty secretary who informed me that Mr. Williams was out of the office at the moment and would be back shortly. I gave her my number and asked her to have him return the call. I leaned back in the swivel chair and pictured the infamous "Vaseline Game" in my mind.

From what I could remember, Davis had been overpowering that day, with a sharp-breaking pitch and sneaky fastball that kept the batters off balance. I had been watching the game from my living room TV, so I was at the mercy of the director's choosing to show Davis on the mound. I remembered the plate umpire, Augie Casillo, walking to the mound and demanding to see Davis' glove. The big pitcher had handed it over confidently, and then exploded in anger when Casillo called over the other members of the crew and they all took turns passing the glove around. The next thing I remembered was that Casillo confiscated the glove and passed it to a representative of the Commissioner's office.

At which Jeff Davis went berserk. He ranted and stormed around the mound. When another glove was given to him, he tossed it twenty feet in the air in anger. Casillo warned him to cut the crap and play ball. That's when Davis went for the arbiter. Three teammates and the rest of the umpiring crew held Davis back, and with an exaggerated hitchhiking gesture, Casillo tossed Davis out of the game.

The ringing phone interrupted my thoughts.

"Don't tell me, Slots, let me guess," Ducky said. "You were shut out for a box seat on opening day and you want me to get you a ticket?"

It was a robust, affable voice, used to the give-and-take of the business world.

"Not even close. How is the big executive these days?" I asked him.

"The only place I'm getting big is around the middle. I've put on thirty pounds since I'm in this job."

"Unlimited expense accounts will do that every time."

We made some small talk and reminisced about some of the characters we'd played with. I finally got around to talking about Davis.

"Yeah, I remember the big jerk. The guy was a bad apple. The best thing that happened for baseball was him getting out of the game."

"I'm trying to get some information about him. I thought maybe you could help me."

There was a pause.

"Wait a second, Slots. Didn't he bean you once? Yeah, I remember, he got you right on the cheek."

"That's the Jeff Davis we know and love. I'm working on something and—"

"What is it, Slots? You're being as tentative as a fat lady on a freshly waxed floor. C'mon, buddy, out with it."

"I'd like to see the files on the Commissioner's hearing on Davis. I need all the stuff that got him suspended from baseball."

"Why?"

"I'm working on a case. My client thinks Davis never doctored the ball and he was innocent of the charges."

"That was three or four years ago. Why the interest now?"

"It's involved."

I pictured Ducky sitting in his office, his feet up on the desk, mulling over my request.

"Sorry, Slots, no can do. What you're asking me to do is to let you have something that's not my property. I like you, buddy boy, but I also like my job. I've got no reason to do anything that might help Davis."

"What if I appeal to your sense of justice?" I lobbed back weakly.

"Appeal all you want, the answer is still no. For all I know, your client could be a hotshot lawyer looking to sue the Commissioner for taking away Davis' livelihood. I'm not betting into that kind of a hand."

53

"My client is a thirteen-year-old kid, Davis' son. He thinks his father's innocent and he's taken a lot of abuse sticking up for the old man."

"Is that on the level?"

"One hundred percent."

"All right, Slots, I'll tell you what I can do. You just sit tight for a moment and I'll be right back."

I held the receiver and got an earful of what was called "easy listening" music. There were strings and flutes dancing around a familiar tune that I was just about to identify when Ducky got back on.

"This is what I can do for you, Slots. I've got the folder right here. You can ask me what you want, but that doesn't mean I'm going to answer."

"Okay."

"Another thing is that I don't get quoted."

"All right. Look it over and refresh your memory and give me your impressions."

"I know this case, Slots. There's no doubt that Davis was using a foreign substance. The whole umpiring crew saw the petroleum jelly on the inside of the glove. I personally saw the glove and it had a handful of goo on the inside palm."

"What else do you have?"

"You've got to be kidding! That's not enough?"

"Maybe he had chapped palms and he wasn't using the stuff on the ball at all."

"Sure, and maybe he just wanted to use it to slick down his Afro," Ducky said sarcastically. "Look, we got supporting evidence from his catcher. Terry Winnegar caught him in the game and told us that after Davis threw a wet one, Terry wiped it off on his uniform and threw it back to him. He said he and Davis had been doing that all season."

"I never heard that before."

"And you didn't hear it now. Winnegar was given immunity by the Commish if he told the truth. It's open and shut, Slots. We interviewed a lot of people and almost nobody had a good word for Davis."

"You said 'almost'—that means someone backed him."

"His pitching coach, Herm Wiley. Wiley said he watched Davis the whole time he was with the team and he never put any foreign substance on the ball. Of course, Wiley was given all the credit for Davis' resurrection from the minors, so he couldn't very well tell the world that his prodigy was using grease."

"It doesn't sound too good."

"Tell the kid to find another cause, Slots. This one's a dead end."

"I'll go through the motions for a little while. Does the league keep a file of home addresses?"

"Yeah, I can get them through the pension office."

"I'll want to interview Winnegar, Casillo, and Wiley. That should wrap it up."

"I can give you Winnegar and Wiley, but Casillo's not in the files."

"Why's that, Dan?"

"About six or eight months after the Davis incident, he quit the game and dropped out of sight."

That perked my interest. "Really?"

"Don't get too excited. It doesn't mean a thing. His wife was terminally ill. He took her down to Mexico to some health facility where she could get laetrile, you know, that apricot derivative."

"I've heard of it."

"Well, he liked it down there and he never came back to the States. He had no kids and his wife finally did die, so there were no ties."

I copied down the two addresses Ducky gave me, and also took Augie Casillo's last residence in Connecticut.

I thanked him and reassured him again that nothing would backfire in his face because of the information he had given me.

6

. . . .

I called Father Quinn and told him what I had found
out, that Davis didn't want to take an active interest in anything but his Scotch, and that according
to Ducky Williams, it was an airtight scenario.

It didn't take Quinn more than a few seconds to digest what I had told him.

I wasn't surprised at his answer. "Keep at it, Slots.
I've got a feeling about this thing. Kick over a few
more stones and let's see what happens."

Herm Wiley's address was in upstate New York, in
Sullivan County. I spoke to his sister, who said Herm
was out hunting and wouldn't be back until supper
time. I explained to her that I was an investigator
working on an important case and it was vital that I
talk to her brother.

"Well then, why not join us for dinner?" she said.
"Herm would love to have the company and I know
he'd be delighted to help."

I tried to get out of the dinner but she wouldn't hear

of it. It was good to be reminded that there were still some nice people in the world. Too often I was exposed to the Jeff Davis types.

I let the Porsche out a few notches on the Thruway and shaved a half hour off the three-hour trip. The sky was turning an ominous metal gray, and a rim of orange sun played peekaboo with a far-off mountain as it set in the west.

Wiley's place was down a dirt road with a simple wooden sign saying WILEY and an arrow pointing the way. A rustic mailbox with its red flag up also had WILEY painted on its side and I followed the fork about three hundred feet until I saw the house.

It was a strong, unimposing, solid wood house. Behind it was a forest, which was taking on an eerie look as dusk set in. A dog lying in the front yard barked at me a couple of times but didn't think I was worth getting up for.

There was no bell, just a heavy brass knocker. A woman who I presumed was Herm's sister answered the door.

"You must be Mr. Resnick," she said in a voice that was now familiar.

"And you are Herm's sister?"

"Yes, I am. I'm a Wiley, too. Jessica is my first name. I never married, just an old maid." She said it with a shrug and a good-natured laugh. "Herm's inside. He was so happy to hear we were having company."

"I hope this isn't a bother."

"None at all," she assured me.

"Herm, this is Mr. Resnick, the investigator I told you about."

"Pleased to meet you," he said, and sounded as if he meant it.

"I'm sorry I didn't give you more notice, but your sister said that it wouldn't be an imposition."

·He waved my words off. "No, no, no. We're pleased as punch to have a guest over. Jessie will have dinner

5 8

set out for us in a little while. In the meantime, what are you drinking?"

I settled on a Strohs and watched Herm pour it into a beer glass. He knew to pour it straight down the center for a broader head.

He took a Coke for himself.

"Doctor's orders. I'm trying to head off an ulcer problem," he explained. "No hard stuff, no spices."

It dawned on me that Herm and his sister would be ringers for the American Gothic couple. Just add twenty pounds on each of the artist's figures and paint in a couple of smiles, and you had Jessica and Herm Wiley.

Appropriately, the house could have been a museum of Early Americana. There were old-fashioned muskets on the wall, carved eagles, pictures of Civil War generals, models of the *Merrimac* and the *Monitor*. On the mantel were at least two dozen replicas of tall-masted ships in bottles.

Herm noticed my looking at them. "That's my hobby, putting those things together."

"You need a lot of patience and a steady hand," I said.

"For me, it's the most relaxing thing in the world. I take my tweezers and my little tools and start buildin' one of those things and the next thing I know, the day is over. Lots of people think the bottles are cut in half and then sealed around the ships. You can see for yourself that these bottles have no seams."

"You build it folded down and then raise the sails inside with little strings, no?"

"Right you are, Mr. Resnick," he said, beaming. "Have a seat and tell me what brings you out of the city to see me."

I sat down in an overstuffed easy chair covered with a floral print, and Herm took the wooden rocker across from me. Jessica disappeared into the kitchen.

"I understand you were the pitching coach for Texas a couple of years back?"

Herm nodded. "Yep, I left them last year after nine years. This spring, I'll be working with the kids in the Boston organization. There's forty-two more days before the pitchers have to report to Florida."

He was about sixty, with clear blue eyes and a weather-beaten face. My guess was that he could have traced his ancestors back to the *Mayflower*, and that he was damned proud of it.

"I'm here to ask you a few questions about Jeff Davis."

He nodded and ran his hands through his sparse gray hair. "He in trouble?" Herm asked.

"No more than usual. This has to do with the play-off game when they tossed him out for loading up the ball."

"How did you know to look me up?" he asked, his eyebrows knitting together. "You know, I'm probably the only fella that spoke up for him during the Commissioner's hearing."

"I know that, that's why I want to talk to you. I'd like to find out what you think happened."

"It doesn't seem to me that it matters a'tall. Not that I won't answer your question, Mr. Resnick, but what's the point of it?"

"My client believes in Davis' innocence and he wants to clear his name."

"I see. A matter of principle, eh? I can respect that."

Jessica appeared at the door. "Dinner is ready, gentlemen. Let's not let it get cold."

"Come, Mr. Resnick, we'll talk inside," Herm said.

The dining room was warm and cozy and filled with the smells of fresh-baked bread and vegetable soup. Herm explained that Jessica just needed an excuse to whip up a company dinner and my call was as good as any.

We had pot roast that had been braised in onion

soup, side plates of broccoli, corn, and potatoes, with cider, apple pie, and ice cream.

I had almost forgotten what good food was like. My usual bill of fare was a burger and a slice of pizza.

I told Jessica how much I had enjoyed the meal and she made me promise to come again. It was obvious that she enjoyed cooking.

"I'll clear the table and let you men finish talking," she said. I offered to help, but she wouldn't hear of it.

Herm had already filled in a lot of the details. He had spotted a number of flaws in Davis' pitching motion when he came to Texas. He started to work with the big guy using video tapes.

"I don't want to get too technical here, Mr. Resnick, but a power pitcher has to use his legs to be effective. Now, because Davis was so strong physically, he was able to get away using his upper torso and shoulder. He wasn't getting any drive from his legs."

"I understand. I played a little ball myself."

"Okay, then you know what I'm talking about. Well, I got Jeff to change his motion."

"He listened to you? I always thought he'd be too stubborn to listen to anyone."

Herm smiled. "I'm talking about the man's bread and butter here, Mr. Resnick. He wasn't that much of a fool. Well, we straightened out his mechanics, but he still wasn't getting anybody out. He was pitching as well as he ever did, but he was getting plastered."

"Why? That doesn't make sense. I hit against the guy and he was throwing BBs. If he regained his form, no one could touch him."

"Mr. Resnick, I've seen all the great ones in my time. I saw Warren Spahn in his last year in pro ball. Believe me, sir, the man was throwing the ball better in his last year than he had ten years before. The key to the decline of a pitcher is control. With age you lose control. All it is is a matter of four inches.

"When you're young, you can nip the black of the

strike zone and the count is no balls and a strike, or oh and two. The pitcher is in the driver's seat. You make a mistake and the hitter has to foul off a pitch and he's still in the hole. Now when you get older, that control leaves you. Now you're off the plate by a couple of inches. The count is two and one, or three and oh. The hitter is sitting on your pitch knowing that if you make a mistake, he walks—and there isn't a pitcher alive who can consistently throw a fastball by a major-league hitter who's sitting on it."

"So you taught Davis the slip pitch."

Herm nodded. He held out his hand and spread out his fingers. "Davis has very long and powerful fingers."

Herm took an apple from the table and placed it between his index and middle fingers. "Now the slipper is held like this, across the seams, and the pitcher throws it like a fastball. The rotation causes it to drop like a stone within a few yards of the plate. Davis tried it a few times and he loved it. We sent him down to the minors to develop it in game situations and he came back up to the bigs a superstar again."

"You never saw him use Vaseline on the ball?"

"I said he never put a foreign substance on the ball. There was no need for him to do that. I never figured out what prompted Augie to come out to the mound. No one on the other team complained. Casillo walked out there on his own to inspect the glove."

"He saw something funny in the way the ball moved," I offered.

"Look, Mr. Resnick, let's say that you were going to throw a loaded ball. When would you do it? Would you do it with no one on base in the beginning of the game, or later in a key situation when you needed an edge? You see what I'm saying? Why would Augie check the glove, and why would Davis do something he never did before? You want to put grease on a ball, you better practice how to throw the damn thing because a spot of grease the size of a dime can make a ball rise two feet above the catcher's head, or kill worms three feet in front of the batter's box. See, it didn't make any sense for Davis to use Vaseline."

"Winnegar said Davis had been doing it the whole season."

"He was lying."

"Did he have a reason?"

Herm laughed. "Listen, you'd have to know Jeff. Nothing he ever did was his own fault. If a hitter got a big hit off him, he'd scream at the catcher. He'd claim the catcher called for the wrong pitch. He was having a running battle with Winnegar all year. He told the manager, Ed Sarner, that he wouldn't pitch if Winnegar was his catcher. It was only after Sarner threatened to fine Jeff that he relented. The two guys had a running battle all year long."

"So you think Winnegar made up a story to get even."

"I wouldn't say telling the truth was one of Terry's strong points," Herm said, winking.

"That still doesn't explain where the grease came from," I said.

"Nope."

"Any theories?"

"Nope, but I can tell you that when Davis cheated he didn't use Vaseline."

"I thought you said Davis didn't put anything on the ball."

"That's right. He didn't use a foreign substance. He didn't need to."

Herm smiled at my confusion.

"Hand me that knife, Mr. Resnick," he said.

He took it from me and put a nick in the skin of the apple, then he folded the skin over.

"That was Davis' trick when the game was on the line. He did it maybe once or twice a game at most. He had this ring with an edge that was as sharp as a razor. In a tight situation he'd walk off the mound, rub up the ball, nick it with the ring and fold it over. That ball could be two feet outside and just whoosh right over the plate. What the hell did he need Vaseline for?"

I got back to the city around midnight. Jessica's heavy dinner and the long monotonous drive had made me tired—too tired to notice the beat-up blue van sitting in the spot next to the fire hydrant outside the door of my office . . . and too tired to see my thin black friend from Smokey's until it was too late.

He jammed a pistol into my left kidney and told me to walk into the office. He was smart enough to keep the gun a few inches off me so I wouldn't give him a replay of the afternoon.

I had trouble finding my keys and that earned me another jab with the barrel.

"I ain't playin' with you, Resnick. Now stop your damn stallin'," he hissed.

I got the door opened and he shoved me inside.

"Can I offer you some coffee?" I asked him.

"Shut up, wiseass. Set yourself down on the couch and keep your mouth shut."

I followed his orders and he pulled up a chair facing me. He straddled it, leaning his body forward, the big gun pointed at the center of my chest. I noticed his head was taped over his right eyebrow where I had banged him into the brick wall. We sat like that, facing each other, for a couple of minutes, with him glaring hatred and me trying to figure out what was going on.

"Look, Slim, I know you're getting a big kick out of this, but frankly I'm starting to get a little bored. Why don't you and me have a couple of beers and talk over the important questions of our time."

"Shut up!"

"I'll start us off. How do you think this country is going to get the balance of trade back in our favor? Do you favor protectionist legislation, or are you one of those traditionalists who believe in the free-market system and no punitive tariffs?"

"I'm gonna blow your fuckin' head off," he warned.

"Okay. I'm not stupid. I can see that current events isn't your forte. Let's talk music. You into rap, Slim, or do you get down with Motown? For my money, you can't beat Smokey Robinson and the Miracles. Who do you like? I got it! You're a Supremes man, right? Sure. Remember them with Diana Ross before she went solo? Hey, Slim, do you think Michael Jackson looks like Diana Ross?"

"I tole you to shut up. Now I'm gonna see how much shit you can talk with your damn throat cut."

He reached into his pants pocket and drew out a switchblade which he flicked to attention. He knew how to hold a knife, palm up, balanced between the thumb and index finger. When you were serious about killing a man, you jabbed into the soft bowel and straight up to the solar plexus. The heart was too well protected by bone, so the stroke was always upward, never down.

He got off the chair and walked toward me. He had me covered with the gun in his left hand and he balanced the menacing knife in his right.

"Okay, Slim, I know why you're sore. Here I am coming up with all the topics and doing so much talking you can't get a word in. I'm big enough to admit when I'm wrong. Go ahead, you start the conversation. Any topic you want to talk about is okay with me."

"The name's not Slim, motherfucker. The name's Pete Dabbs. I want you to remember that when you're dying."

He brought his hand back, ready to stab forward. It was either the knife or the bullet, but luckily I didn't have to make that choice.

"Hold it!"

We both looked over to the door. Jeff Davis was standing there, his broad shoulders filling the doorway.

"Put that damn toothpick away, Pete, you damn fool. I told you to hold him for me, not to kill him."

"Shit, Jeff, I was just going to scare him a little."

65

"Bullshit! Now get the hell out of here."

"Hey, man," Dabbs whined, "I owe him a little something for this." He pointed to the bandages on his head.

"You just do what I tell you, man!" Davis said icily.

Dabbs reluctantly folded his knife and backed off. "I get you another time, baby," he said, walking toward the door.

"Nice talking to you," I replied.

Davis waited for Dabbs to leave and then turned back to me. He looked tired, beads of perspiration balanced on his smooth black skull. He took the chair Dabbs had occupied and reached in his shirt pocket for a pack of Marlboros. Even sitting in the chair he was as big as a house. He made a production of lighting the cigarette and then blew smoke into the air.

"You shouldn't be playin' with Pete that way. He got a hell of a temper."

"I don't know what happened to my manners. I'll write him a note of apology."

Davis ignored me and stared at the lit end of his butt. "You asked me something this afternoon, about what happened during the game in that play-off."

"Yeah."

"Well, I'll give you your answer, if you're still interested."

"I'm interested."

"I'll tell you what you want to know, Resnick, and then you stay out of my life."

He shifted in the chair and brought his face close to mine. I could smell the booze on his breath.

"Everything they said about me was true. I figured I needed an insurance policy, so I loaded up my glove with Vaseline. That's it! That's the whole story."

He seemed nervous and unsure of himself. I wasn't buying it.

"Somehow it doesn't ring true. I can't see Jeff Davis needing an insurance policy. You were on a roll, winning the last six games you pitched and three of them by shutouts. You were up against a team composed of Punch and Judy singles hitters. I just can't see the mighty Jeff Davis quaking in his boots."

He smiled to himself and shook his head. "What the hell do you know about pressure, man? What the hell do you know about standing in front of sixty thousand people and a hundred million more on TV? Every pitch you throw can mean whether you get into the World Series or not. Every one of your teammates is depending on you. Shit, Resnick, that's the whole story. I got caught, and that's it. Don't make no more out of it. I'm livin' with this thing for three years now and I don't need it dug up again by you."

"How come Herm Wiley thinks you were framed?"

That caught him by surprise.

"He's a jackass!" Davis fumed.

"He made a lot of sense to me. He said you had a different trick if you needed a sure out. Something about cutting the ball with your ring."

Davis' face tightened in anger.

"Well, this one time out I used grease. Look, you just stay out of my business!"

He wagged his finger at me. "You can have it any way you want. You want trouble, I'll give you trouble like you never seen. On the other hand, if you want to be reasonable . . ."

He tossed a wad of bills at me, wrapped by a rubber band. I picked it up and noted they were all hundreds.

"You got three thousand there. I don't want you to lose your fee, Resnick. You keep that money and be smart. You keep stickin' your nose in my face and I'm going to chop it off. This ain't no joke to me, unnerstand?"

I tossed the bills back at him. "I've already got a client, a thirteen-year-old kid who believes in his dad."

There was no reaction, except Davis took a deep drag on his smoke. "The boy got to learn there ain't no

Santa Claus, and Superman is a jiveass in long underwear."

He put the money back in his pocket. "All I can say to you, man, is you were warned."

He got up and walked to the door.

"Davis!" I called after him. "You want me to back off, then give me a reason. No threats, no money, just a good reason."

He froze, his hand on the doorknob, then he turned around.

"Okay, man, I'll tell you the reason. I been out of the game for three years. Come two more and I'll be eligible for the Hall of Fame voting. I got all the statistics I need . . . no-hitter, perfect games, tied for most strikeouts in a game, Cy Young Award. There ain't more than two, maybe three pitchers in the history of the game got better stats than me.

"Except that ain't what the sportswriters going to think about when my name comes up voting time. They just going to remember that last game and throw everything else I done out the window. I figure in two more years, the Vaseline Game is gonna get less attention and my record will be looked at more carefully. That is, if nobody starts stirrin' around in the ashes and starts the fire up again.

"Bein' in the Hall of Fame means big money to me. There's endorsements and commercials and appearances. Shit, man, I don't want you or anybody else screwing up my chances.

"I hear you keep up with this thing, and what I done to your jaw before gonna seem just like a little ole mosquito bite."

He slammed the door behind him.

7

. . . .

I called for a client conference.

The morning found me sitting in Theda's cheery kitchen with Arthur and Harry Quinn listening to a rundown of the past twenty-four hours. Theda flitted about serving up a breakfast of flapjacks and bacon.

I told them about my conversation with Herm Wiley and watched the excitement in Arthur's face as the prospect loomed that Jeff hadn't doctored the ball. The boy grew more thoughtful when I told them how Davis had asked me to stay out of his way because of the Hall of Fame possibility. I left out the threats and the money that was offered, and I saw no reason to mention the "ring trick." Nothing would be gained by busting the kid's balloon. "So, guys, it's up to you. Do we go ahead with the investigation, or pack it in?" I asked.

Harry Quinn shrugged. "I guess he has a point about the Hall of Fame, Arthur. He did tell Slots he was guilty."

"But Herm Wiley said it wasn't true," the boy countered.

"Why would Jeff lie about it, son?" Harry asked gently.

Theda filled each of our plates with what was left of the pancake stack.

"Mom, what do you think?" Arthur asked.

"I'm a prejudicial witness, so you can't get me involved. You men make the decisions, and whatever it is, I'll go along."

"Slots, if Mr. Wiley was right, then that would clear my dad and he'd have no trouble getting into the Hall of Fame, right?" Arthur looked at me with those large questioning eyes.

"That's right, but if he did it, then it would just open up all the old wounds."

"I'm afraid the best thing to do is to let sleeping dogs lie," Father Quinn said sadly. "You have to believe the man's confession. If he maintained his innocence, then I'd be the first to want to follow up on it, but . . ."

I watched the kid wrestle with himself. He wanted so much to be able to help his father, he had built up a whole fantasy about it. In his mind, he'd help prove his dad's innocence, Jeff would be returned to superstar status, and the kids in school would have to eat their words. Maybe then Theda and Jeff would get together again and he'd have a real family.

It wasn't an easy dream to let go of, not if you were a lonely kid without friends and needing some fatherly affection.

"What do you think we ought to do, Slots?" he asked me.

I thought it over. There were a few things that didn't add up, and verbalizing them might help. I'd found Herm Wiley to be very knowledgeable and a lot of things he had said made sense. The one thing that was constant on any baseball team was the close relationship between a pitcher and the team's pitching coach. The coach was mother hen, father confessor, and psychologist for every one of the athletes he worked with. If Herm Wiley didn't know Davis, then no one knew him.

"I think there's enough doubt to warrant looking into this a little deeper," I said. "Wiley made a good point about how difficult it would be to control a ball with Vaseline on it if you had never done it before. Jeff told me himself that he did it only on that one day."

"Didn't Terry Winnegar, the catcher, say he was doing it all season?" Harry asked.

"Yes, that puts Terry's story directly contrary to Wiley's and even contradicts Jeff's confession."

"If you dig further, what's your next step, Slots?" Father Quinn wanted to know.

"I'd like to interview Casillo, the umpire, but he seems to have vanished. So that leaves Terry Winnegar."

I brought out a piece of paper with Winnegar's address on it. "He lists a gas station as his mailing location. It's on Route 80 in Jersey."

"Can I go with you, Slots? Please . . ."

My first reaction was to say no, but there was something so compelling in the way the kid asked that I threw it back to Theda.

"That's up to your mother," I told him.

"Mom, please, can I? Can I go with Slots?"

"I guess so. It won't be dangerous, will it?"

"I doubt it, and besides, I got the feeling that Arthur can take care of himself in a tough situation. Am I right?"

"Yeah. You bet!"

The kid had a smile a yard long.

The address for Terry Winnegar that Ducky had given me turned out to be Winnegar's Gas Station & Auto Repair Shop. It was an eighty-mile trip, about two hours from midtown.

Along the way, Arthur and I finally broke through the conversational wall. He wanted to know all about being a detective and he asked me the inevitable question: "Did ya ever have to kill anybody?"

The fact was that I'd had to use my gun twice during my tenure on the force, and both times it had been a question of him or me. If you're any kind of human being at all, you carry that baggage with you all through your life. You go over the situations in your mind. You find yourself daydreaming, staring off into space. You're haunted by the thought that perhaps there might have been another way, that maybe there had been an option that you'd overlooked.

Shooting a man with a gun is nothing like dropping a bomb on a little strip of land with sterile cross hairs on a green radarscope. It's the tearing asunder of flesh, bone, and sinew. It's hearing the choking cry of agony and seeing the still-pumping arteries fountain blood into the air. It's having to face the dead man's relatives and children.

Killing a man meant questions, interrogations, investigations, and dozens of hours of paperwork. It meant mentally taking hold of yourself and finally coming to the realization that there was no choice. Pulling the trigger was the right thing to do. When the investigations are over and the second-guessers and bureaucrats finally get around to clearing your name and everybody agrees it was the proper action, there are still some nights when you wake up and wonder.

"Yeah, Arthur. Two times. Both times if I hadn't fired, they would have killed me."

"Wow! That is neat!"

"Hey, Arthur," I said, changing the subject, "how about you and me playing 'count the license plates'? Let's see who can spot more out-of-state license plates, any state except New York and New Jersey."

"Okay, you're on."

By the time we got to Winnegar's, I was leading ten to eight. Both of us laughed at one out-of-state plate from Alaska that said "Brrr."

The station was one of those modern jobs, lots of

glass and lights and three islands holding three pumps on each. There was an attendant on each island working out of an all-weather booth, pumping the gas and checking the oil. He rang up the cash in the booth, or ran the credit cards through the machine. Behind the gas pumps was the repair shop with four bays, each occupied with a car on the lift, and attached to the shop was the main office.

I pulled the Porsche over to a corner of the station where it would be out of the way and I told Arthur he'd have to wait for me there. He looked a little disappointed, so I cautioned him that if I wasn't back in fifteen minutes, he was to get the State Troopers.

He looked at me very seriously until I couldn't hold back a smile and he knew I was putting him on.

"You're foolin' with me, Slots," he said, smiling.

I gave him a mock jab on the jaw and told him I'd be back as soon as I could.

I've always been semi-invisible in gas stations. By that I mean that whenever I've gone into a station with a car problem, everyone always seems to be too busy to see me. I find myself waiting around politely for this mechanic or that mechanic to lift his head from under the hood, but even when they do it's to help some guy with overalls and a "CAT" cap with the brim turned around.

This time I walked into the office to find some grizzled yokel reading a tabloid with the headline: "Alien Family Astounds Scientists." Inquiring minds want to know, I figured. Naturally, he never looked up from the paper and I finally had to tap him on the shoulder to get some recognition.

"I'm looking for Terry Winnegar," I told him.

"Who're you?"

"Name's Resnick. I'm an investigator."

There was an FM squawk box on the desk, and Gabby Hayes pushed down the button.

"Some fella here to see Terry. His name's Remmick and he's a cop."

It was close enough, I decided, so I didn't bother correcting him.

"Send him back," a voice barked.

"Back" was a long white corridor past a broom closet and a bathroom and leading to a door marked NO ADMITTANCE. I knocked and the door opened a crack, and then all the way.

It was a small square room without any windows; the ventilation was coming from a single duct with several ribbons tied to the grille. There were six different TV monitors on the first level of the wall and an additional six monitors on a shelf above those. Each of the monitors had a different view of the station. Three of the feeding cameras were positioned over each of the cash registers in the outside booths, there were other long shots of each island, and the final cameras were sending back pictures from the auto bays and cash register.

Two men were sitting at a table staring at the monitors, in between playing knock rummy. One of the men was enormously fat. He seemed to ooze flesh from a mountainous, shapeless body that spilled over a very sturdy-looking La-Z-Boy. He wore a short-sleeved pajamalike top over homemade pants fastened by a piece of white clothesline. The playing cards in his hamhock hands looked like postage stamps.

The other man, who had opened the door and then reclaimed his seat at the table, was the short, stocky Terry Winnegar. There wasn't another chair in the room, so I stood.

"What's your problem?" Winnegar asked me as he picked up a jack the fat man had thrown away.

"I'd like to talk to you about Jeff Davis and the play-off game you caught him in."

"Is that right?" Winnegar said snottily. He smiled at the fat man. "Hear that, Tiny? The man wants to talk about Jeff Davis."

Tiny thought that was funny and his whole body Jell-O'd as he laughed.

Winnegar joined in with a high-pitched cackle. "You a cop or something?" he asked, throwing down an ace.

"I'm an investigator," I said.

"Well, shit! Ain't I impressed. You impressed, Tiny?"

Tiny laughed again as he shook his head no.

"Looks like you found yourself a great audience, Winnegar. Now I'm sure I could stand here and amuse you fellows all day long but you've got this important game to get on with and I wouldn't want you to miss seeing any of your help pocket a few quarters on the tube. Why don't you be a nice guy and answer a few simple questions for me?"

"He wants me to answer some questions," Winnegar told Tiny. "He must think I'm stupid."

He turned to me. "Is that it, mister? You think I'm stupid?"

"You are stupid, Terry," Tiny said in a high-pitched eunuch voice. He started laughing again. Talk about your jolly fat people . . .

"Yeah, maybe I am, I got you working for me.

"Now look, Mr. Investigator, I got nothing to say to you. Don't waste my time. The door is right behind you."

"That's not very friendly," I told him.

He shrugged. "So the girls won't vote me Miss Congeniality."

Tiny fairly shrieked with laughter.

"Just a couple of fast questions, and I'm gone!"

"Look, you don't seem to understand. I told the Commissioner everything I know. If you want to hear more, you got to come up with the green. I'll sell you my story for a minimum of five figures. You got that money on you? I don't think so, so good-bye. Don't slam the door on your way out."

I fought down the urge to throttle Winnegar and made a quick about-face out of the office. A man has the right in his own place of business to talk or not to talk to anyone he pleases. I wasn't very happy about it, especially with Arthur ready to hang on to any thread of hope, but that's how it goes sometimes.

"What did he say, Slots?" Arthur asked me as I climbed into the Porsche next to him.

"We struck out, kid. He wouldn't answer any questions."

Arthur slumped down in the seat, his chin drooping, his eyes blinking away tears.

"Hey, c'mon, champ. We'll come up with something else."

The trouble was I couldn't think of what that something else might be. With Winnegar tight as a clam, and Casillo dropping off the face of the earth, there didn't seem to be many avenues to follow.

We'd driven about fifteen minutes before Arthur snapped out of his gloom. "Thanks for trying anyway," he said softly.

"You okay now?"

"Uh-huh."

Taking the kid along hadn't been such a hot idea after all. In fact, taking on the damn case hadn't been such a hot idea.

"You want to continue the license-plate game?" Arthur asked.

"Okay. It's ten to eight, my favor."

"Nope, I got four more," he said, smiling. "Four of the cars in the station were out of state."

"Is that on the level?"

"Yup."

"Okay, twelve to ten, yours."

We'd driven along another ten minutes before what the kid had said sank in. "Arthur, those four out-of-state plates at Winnegar's, were they getting gas?"

"No, Slots. I couldn't see the pumps from where we were parked. They were in the repair shop."

Bingo!

I pulled off at the next exit and turned the car back in the western direction. It was a long shot, but from what I'd seen of Terry Winnegar, the odds were dropping fast.

"We going back, Slots?"

"We're going back, Arthur. Something you said might make a big difference in Mr. Winnegar's attitude."

"Something I said? Wow!"

"Look, Arthur, don't get your hopes up. It's just a theory. Okay?"

"Okay."

I drove back to Winnegar's and pulled off on the side of the road about sixty feet from the station. I had Arthur open the glove compartment and pull out my Bausch & Lomb binocs and my Nikon. We had a good view of the three gas pumps on the island closest to us. We couldn't see the second island because of the angle, and the third island was also obstructed. We would have to concentrate on the three nearest pumps.

"What are we going to do, Slots?"

"Detective work, Arthur. The most important tools a detective has are—"

"His gun and his disguises," Arthur offered.

"Nope, his ability to watch carefully, and to wait."

"What are we watching and waiting for, Slots?"

I handed him the binoculars. "Watch those three gas pumps for any car that has an out-of-state license plate."

"What has that—"

"You'll see. Just do what I tell you."

It took five minutes for the first out-of-stater to pull up for gas. The driver was a young man about twenty who stepped out of the car and watched the attendant pump in ten dollars' worth.

"So what am I looking for?" Arthur wanted to know.

"My guess is an out-of-state car with either women, or maybe an elderly couple. Just keep your eyes peeled."

I checked out the four bays and every car there had

an out-of-state plate. I wondered what the odds were on that.

As we waited, Terry's mechanics finished up with two cars. One they drove off to a side parking spot, the other they gave to an elderly man, who drove off.

Another half hour went by.

"Here comes one," Arthur said.

It was an '80 Grand Prix from Missouri, carrying a woman and a small child.

"This could be it," I told him.

I got the Nikon ready with the zoom lens on. "Now tell me everything you see the attendant doing."

"He's just giving her gas . . . now he's raising the hood and looking at the engine. He's leaning over . . ."

"He's checking the oil," I told Arthur.

My zoom picked up everything Arthur was seeing. "Now what?" I asked.

"He's checking the tires and putting air in."

I started clicking away with the Nikon.

"Watch closely, Arthur. There, what did you see?"

"He like threw something under the car," Arthur said, very surprised.

"It looked like that. What he did was take a squeeze bottle from his back pocket, sprayed under the car, and then he put the bottle back in his pocket."

I had captured the whole sequence down on film.

Now the attendant was pointing to a spot under the car and talking to the woman. She looked very disturbed and he shrugged his shoulders. He pointed to the repair shop, and in a few minutes the woman got back in the car and drove to one of the open bays.

"It's an old trick, Arthur. You have people making long car rides and you frighten them into getting their cars fixed even though there's nothing wrong with them."

"Yeah, but how?" Arthur wanted to know.

"When the pump jockey bent down to put air in the tire, he pulled out a squeeze bottle filled with oil. Then he squirted it under the engine and told the lady he noticed a leak. When she looked under the car, there was the dripping oil. Then the attendant says that if he were her, he wouldn't go much farther because a leak like that could ruin the whole car. He tells her to bring it into the shop so they can put it on the lift. Once they do that, they can ask anything they want to fix something that's perfectly fine in the first place."

"Man, that's dirty!"

"Yeah, but thanks to your sharp eyes, we've got a chance to make Mr. Winnegar a little more cooperative. Hang out here, Arthur. I shouldn't be long."

I walked down the road onto the concrete of the station and right up to the attendant, who was sitting in his booth reading a girlie magazine.

"What can I do for you, Ace?" he asked as I stepped into the booth.

"You can give me the little article you're carrying in the back pocket of your uniform," I said evenly.

"What the hell are you talking about?"

"I'm talking about the little squeeze bottle that squirts oil under the engine."

He swallowed hard and stood up. "Are you a cop?"

"Nope. That means I don't have to worry about breaking your arm if I have to. The way I see it, you just work for the man and you do as you're told. There's no reason for you to have a problem with me. One way or the other, I'm going to get that bottle, and if I have to hurt you, that's okay too."

"You're right, mister. I just follow orders. I make a few bucks every time I land a fish. Winnegar gives me twenty bucks. I mean, that ain't worth any trouble, a stinkin' twenty bucks here and there."

"That's just how I see it," I told him.

He reached behind him and came out with the rubber squeeze bottle.

"You're a lot smarter than you look," I told him.

I leaned over the register and stuck my face in the camera. "Hey Terry, look what I found." I held up the bottle. "I'm coming back to see you," I said with a wave.

I walked past the man in the office and into the hallway, where Tiny squeezed past me. I noted with some satisfaction that the fat man wasn't laughing anymore. In fact, he kept his eyes down as he slipped past me on his way to the outer office.

The door was open this time and Terry sat at the table facing me. I closed the door behind me and sat down opposite him.

"What did you say your name was?" he asked.

"Resnick."

I put the squeeze bottle on the table. Winnegar stared at it and scratched his cheek.

"What the hell is that thing?" he asked me.

"I found it on your attendant outside. He gives a squirt here and there and Winnegar's gets to do a three-hundred-dollar motor job."

"You must be kidding! My people would never do a thing like that. Since you got that camera around your neck, I suppose you took shots of what you claim happened. Well, I'm really glad you brought this to my attention. That man will be fired immediately. I run a very clean operation here, Mr. Resnick."

"You're a scam artist, Winnegar. I could call Consumer Affairs and they'd close you down in ten seconds. All they would have to do is look at your records and check the addresses of most of your repair customers. If you fudged that up, the tax boys at the IRS have all the time in the world to put together a case on you."

"Get outta here! You've got nothin' but some pictures that you claim shows Jerry doing something to one car."

"Hey, Terry, how far on loyalty do you think your twenty bucks will carry you? When they put those guys on the stand and swear them in and explain the perjury laws, you think they'll lie for you? Your man already told me he was just following your orders."

"Shit!"

Winnegar looked like a cornered animal.

"What the hell do you want to keep your mouth shut?"

"The scam stops as of this moment."

He stared at me, made an angry face, and punched in a button on the squawk box. "Tony, get all the cars out of the bays."

Tony said something that I couldn't make out, but Terry understood.

"You heard me! All of them! Tell them there's no charge . . . everything's on the house today."

"WhatdoItell'em?" came over the box.

"I don't give a shit what you tell them. Tell them it's our anniversary and everything's free."

He released the button.

"I was never comfortable with that shit in the first place. I mean, you see what we got here? This place is a gold mine legitimately. I listened to Tiny. He's my partner but he's always looking for more and more."

"Especially in the refrigerator," I cracked.

Terry didn't think it was funny. In fact, he seemed to have lost that wonderful sense of humor he'd displayed only an hour or so ago.

"Now what?" he asked me.

"Now give me some straight answers about Davis and the celebrated Vaseline Game."

"What do you want to know? Everything I said is on tape in the Baseball Commissioner's office. I told them everything."

"You told them what they wanted to hear," I said forcefully.

"Look, Resnick, I'm not recanting anything. Spring training starts in a couple of months and I got a good shot as backup to Samuels on the Cleveland club. I don't want the Commissioner's office to get pissed at me. I know about biting the hand that feeds me."

"This is just between you and me."

"How can I believe that?"

"You can't, but you can believe that if you don't level with me, I'll go after your ass with everything I've got. That includes the pictures, my interview with your worker, and the testimony of an independent witness who's sitting in my car at this moment."

"Okay—okay, don't read me the fuckin' riot act." He visibly sagged in his chair. "What do you want to know?"

"Jeff Davis never had Vaseline on the ball in any other game during the season. Right?"

"Yeah."

"How did it get in his glove during the play-off game?"

"Hey, hold on, Resnick. I saw a chance to bury the bastard, and believe me, the man is a bastard, but nobody framed that son of a bitch. They caught him with jelly on that day, and nobody can deny that."

"Why did Augie go and check him?"

"I don't know, ask Augie."

"Were there any complaints from the hitters?"

Winnegar shrugged. "I don't remember."

I grabbed him by the shirt collar. "You better remember, pal. You better remember every goddamned detail."

I lifted him off the chair and then shoved him back.

"Okay, okay, take it easy—take it easy. No, nobody really complained. I mean, there was the usual bitching on close pitches, but nobody asked to check the ball."

"Why did Casillo go out to the mound then?"

"Look, Resnick, people were always making accusations about Davis. Maybe Augie saw something he didn't like. That's all I know. Honest."

"Let me get this straight. As far as you know, Davis didn't doctor the ball during the season, and he didn't use a wet one during the play-off game."

"Yeah, that's right. You promised, though, that that's just between us."

I tossed him my card. "If you remember anything else, call me. In the meantime, I'm going to have this place watched. You pull any of that oil-leak stuff and you'll be catching for the penitentiary team at Rahway."

8

. . . .

Sometimes an investigation takes on the earmarks of an accountant's ledger. On the minus side were Davis' own confession and the physical evidence of the Vaseline in the glove. On the plus side were Herm Wiley's intimate knowledge of Davis and the unlikelihood of the pitcher's trying something in the play-offs that he hadn't done all season long. Corroborating Wiley was Winnegar's admission that he had never caught a greased-up ball all season, and that, contrary to what he told the Commissioner's office, he hadn't caught a wet one during the play-off game.

Augie Casillo was another factor that had to be figured in.

When I got back to my office I called Ducky again and got him to read over the testimony given at the hearing. Casillo had stated that he saw Davis step off the mound to rub up the ball and that he seemed to reach for something in his glove. It was an awkward movement, and the ball broke very sharply down and in when it was pitched. The hitter managed to foul the pitch back and the ball went into the stands, but Augie was prompted by Davis' previous actions to look at the inside of his glove.

"Ducky, let me ask you something completely off the record."

"Shoot."

"After this happened, Davis screamed to anyone who would listen to him that he was being framed. I remember him on talk shows, in magazines, on the radio. He'd even grab passersby in the street to hear his side of it."

"That's true."

"Then all of a sudden he goes silent and not another word comes out of him. It was as if someone had told him to keep his mouth shut. Now he readily admits that he was guilty and he's concerned that the incident not be brought up again for fear it'll blow his shot at the Hall of Fame."

"How do you read it, Slots?"

"I'm just throwing a line in the water here, Ducky. What if the Commissioner's office made some kind of deal with him to clam up and take his lumps and they'd see if some sportswriters' arms could be twisted for the Hall of Fame vote?"

"Slots, if anything like that was going on and coming out of this shop, then believe me, I'd know about it. And for the record, I've never heard a word. Quite frankly, we all felt that Davis was bad for baseball. He isn't exactly the image we want to project to the kids of America, but—take this to the bank, Slots—there was no deal."

"Okay, Ducky, no insult intended."

"None taken, Slots. Let me tell you something else. There isn't a chance in the world of Davis' being voted into the Hall in his first year of eligibility. He never made friends with the press, and on top of that, the finding of the Vaseline has tainted all of his pitching achievements. He may have a shot five or ten years down the road, but he's fooling you, and maybe himself, if he thinks he's going to be considered now."

"Okay, Ducks, thanks."

"Anytime, Slots old man."

Ducky had closed the one door I thought had some promise, but he'd pointed out the importance of the testimony of Augie Casillo. The senior umpire was the only person to claim actually to have seen Davis load up the baseball. His was the pivotal testimony, and he was the only witness I hadn't been able to interview.

The phone rang. It was Theda thanking me for taking Arthur with me.

"Slots, for the first time in months he's animated and acting like a real kid instead of a grumpy old man."

"He's a heck of a good kid. I just hope we're not building him up for a fall," I told her.

"I know, I thought of that too. I think we'll just have to take that chance. Anything's better than the way he was."

I hoped she was right.

Augie Casillo's house was on a third of an acre in Manchester, Connecticut. The whole tract of land had been gouged out of a forest and the development was called Sleepy Hollow Homes.

I passed four attractive houses with well-manicured lawns, whose price range I guessed to be from a half to a million bucks, but with the real estate boom in the Northeast, the price might be double that.

Casillo's house might have fit in with the rest at one time, but today it stuck out like a nun at an orgy. It was a two-story wood-and-stucco colonial, large, but completely run down. The front lawn was overrun by weeds and the iron gate leading to the front door was leaning on its side and orange with rust.

I walked up the front stairs to the porch, which had

missing wooden slats and stank from mildew. The door was sealed by two crossed two-by-fours nailed into the frame. The windows on the first floor were also boarded up. On the second floor, the windows still had the jagged edges of glass left by the rocks that had crashed through their centers. But it was just a question of time before all the glass was gone.

I read the notice stapled to the front door. It was a Sheriff's Notice that the property had been claimed by the Town of Manchester for failure to pay back taxes.

I entertained the idea of prying off one of the window boards but thought better of it. The scavengers had already been through this house, and after three years whatever wasn't cemented down would be gone.

The road I'd driven up on was called Sleepy Hollow Road, and true to its name, I hadn't seen another car since I pulled off the Interstate. Now I heard the purr of an automobile and watched as a gold 450 Mercedes pulled up behind the Porsche.

A woman got out of the driver's seat, pulled off her leather driving gloves and waved.

"Hello, there."

"Hello."

"Are you interested in the house?" she called.

I walked down the pathway toward her. "In a manner of speaking. I'm really more interested in the Casillos."

I watched a flicker of surprise cross her eyes. "Oh, did you know Augie and Theresa?"

"Not really, but I would like to talk to Augie."

"You and a lot of other people," she said cryptically. She held out her hand. "I'm Cynthia Marsh."

"Mickey Resnick. They usually call me Slots."

"Well, Slots, I'm the next house down the road. Would you care to stop in for some coffee? Perhaps I could help you."

"That's very kind of you. Lead the way."

We climbed into our cars and I followed Cynthia about a half mile down the road.

She was a stunning woman in her late twenties, model-thin and mostly legs. Her hair, which was raven black, was cut in a severe style that on another woman would have been too masculine. On Cynthia, it just brought out her prominent cheekbones and piercing green eyes. I noticed the diamonds on her fingers and the ranch mink that she wore over a pair of designer jeans.

From the way she talked and moved, I guessed that Cynthia had been around money a long time. Kept women never had that air of total confidence. I figured she'd been born into wealth and married into more. Her home did little to dispel that impression. This one had to sell for at least two million, and you had to have an opinion about it. Either you hated it, or loved it.

It was a concrete bunker with a dome, reminiscent of the Guggenheim Museum in New York. There were no windows and no doors. I followed Cynthia's Mercedes around the circular front and parked behind her.

She was waiting for a comment when I stepped out of my car.

"Is it a house or a flying saucer?" I asked.

She laughed good-naturedly. "I've heard worse descriptions. The people who hate it call it the Marsh Mausoleum. Come with me around back; looks can be deceiving."

I saw what she meant. From the front, it would appear that the concrete went full circle. It didn't. It was actually a semicircle, with the entire back wall of the house made of glass. It extended the width of the house, about one hundred and fifty feet.

Cynthia punched a series of numbers into a key pad, and a plate-glass panel rose up like a garage door to admit us. An electric eye told the mechanism there was no one else coming, so the door retracted.

"The whole house is electronic. We had to have the utility company put in special lines just for us."

"Us?"

"My husband Jeremy and me. He's been involved

with some kind of merger or acquisition—I can't keep track anymore—all I know is he's hardly ever home." There was a note of bitterness, which she shrugged away. "I guess he has to have his outlets, too."

She didn't realize the pun and I let the remark pass.

I followed her into the living room, leaving a trail in the white llama rug. The room was all leather and chrome and splotched with sunlight, which filtered through the thick branches of the trees outside. The effect of the room made you feel that you were sitting in the forest.

"This is lovely," I told her.

"It's so much prettier when the trees are covered with leaves. How do you take your coffee?"

"Don't go to any bother."

"It's no bother at all."

She pressed a button on a console near the white leather couch.

"Betty, fix us some coffee. I'll have mine the usual way, and . . ."

"Black, no sugar."

"Black, no sugar, for my guest. Thanks, dear."

"Are all the rooms facing the forest?"

"Yes," she said with some amusement. "You're wondering how we can get any privacy."

"As a matter of fact, I was."

"That's the question everyone asks."

She pointed to a well-disguised line in the ceiling, hidden from view by a piece of ornate molding.

"You see, we have recessed curtains. I simply press a button, and instant privacy."

She pushed a button on the same console and I heard the hum of a motor. A dark, opaque curtain was slowly being lowered. She pushed the button again and it went back up.

"This house is extraordinary."

"Thank you. You know, you can do a lot with the Casillo house, too. I don't know if you're considering buying the house, but the property alone is worth the money they're asking."

"It seems strange that Augie would just allow the house to be auctioned off in a Sheriff's disposal."

"I'm sure he has his reasons. Oh, here's Betty."

Betty turned out to be a dark-skinned woman dressed in a servant's white uniform, carrying our coffee and finger rolls on a silver serving tray.

"Did Jeremy call?" Cynthia asked her.

"No, mum, he didn't."

I detected the lilt of the Caribbean in her speech.

"All right, dear. That will be all."

Betty gave a half-nod and quietly slipped out of the room.

"Well, Mr. Resnick, I must admit you've piqued my curiosity. If you're not here to purchase the house, may I ask your interest in the Casillos? You, see, we've been hoping, all the homeowners, that is, that someone would buy that place and fix it up. It's just dragging down all our property values in the condition it's in."

"I wish I could help you out, but I'm afraid I'm not here for that. I was hoping to get some idea where Casillo might be. I'm an investigator, and it's important that I talk to Augie about a case I'm working on."

"Oh my, that sounds exciting. So few exciting things happen around here."

She held my eyes with hers an extra second before she flashed her smile.

I wouldn't have been human if I wasn't aware of the way her nipples poked against the white silk of her blouse. I wouldn't have been human if I wasn't aware of the heady perfume she was wearing. I wouldn't have been human if I didn't notice the way her hand rested on my wrist after handing me the cup of coffee.

I was feeling very human.

"You don't look very bored," I told her.

"I try to find ways to occupy my time, but for the most part I feel like a caged tiger. My husband is a much older man, and there are certain . . . shall I say drawbacks, to our marriage."

The hand on my wrist was moving up my arm.

"Am I making you nervous?" she purred.

"I'd hate to spill the coffee all over a white rug."

"Let me take it from you then."

She placed it back on the silver tray and stood up. Her eyes locked into mine as she slowly undid the buttons of her blouse and tossed it on the couch.

I picked up her cue and drew her to me. We settled down on the rug. Her hands were tugging at my shirt and I was pulling off her jeans.

"Betty?"

"She won't come in unless I call her," Cynthia said huskily. "Hurry, please hurry."

We made love hard and fast, our bodies moving at different rhythms, trying to mesh but lost in a lustful hunger that overrode everything.

We finally pulled away, catching our collective breaths and sharing a smile of lazy contentment.

The second time was better. We moved in concert, our bodies entwined and moving as one. We rode the waves and crested powerfully together.

I looked over at Cynthia. Her eyes were closed, a beatific smile on her lips. I closed my own eyes for a second. I must have dozed.

"Miz Marsh, Miz Marsh . . . get up!"

It was Betty, shaking Cynthia awake.

"What . . . what is it?"

"Hurry, your husband is home."

"For God's sake, Betty, head him off," Cynthia said, springing to her feet.

She was dressed in two blinks of an eye and I was just a shade behind her. Betty had done her job well, because by the time Jeremy Marsh stepped into the living room, I was sipping cold coffee and making small talk with Cynthia.

My preconception of Jeremy Marsh had been way

off. When Cynthia had mentioned her husband being involved with mergers and acquisitions, it had brought to mind a hard-driving, cigar-chomping businessman. Instead, Jeremy Marsh was a quiet, dignified man in his sixties.

"Darling, this is Mr. Resnick. Mr. Resnick, my husband, Jeremy."

"I'm so pleased to meet you," he said in a voice that was hardly more than a whisper.

He was impeccably dressed in a blue pinstripe suit, white silk shirt, and a very correct blue-and-gray-striped tie. Jeremy had a full head of white hair that was a stark contrast to his deeply tanned skin.

"They call you Slots, don't they?" he said, shaking my hand.

Cynthia looked surprised. "You two know each other?"

"We've never met," I said. "You've been away on vacation, haven't you? I also think you've been doing some sail-yacht racing."

"Did you tell him that, Cynthia?"

"No, not a word. Why didn't you tell me you knew my husband, Slots?"

"I don't. Your husband pulled his car behind my Porsche and read SLOTS from the license plate."

Jeremy smiled. "My trick was easy. How did you accomplish yours?"

"The tan and the handshake. The tan tells me you've been in a vacation climate; the hard, calloused hand says tough manual work. Since I don't see you as a bricklayer or ditchdigger, it would have to be some sport that toughened your palm. You're a man of means, which made me think of a yacht and rigging sails that would account for the calluses."

Jeremy nodded his approval. "Bravo, Mr. Resnick, well done. I've been away to St. Thomas and managed to get in some sailing time."

"Darling, Mr. Resnick is interested in the Casillos. He's a private investigator."

I thought I saw a look pass between Jeremy and his wife. It happened so fast, I wasn't sure.

I turned to Cynthia. "Mrs. Marsh, you mentioned that a lot of people would like to find Augie Casillo. Why would that be?"

Cynthia looked at her husband. "Why don't you tell him?"

"Mr. Casillo had the regrettable habit of borrowing money and not paying it back. Even more regrettably, I happen to be one of those he borrowed from. I imagine there were others. What's your interest in this, Mr. Resnick?"

"There was an incident in a baseball game a few years back that Augie was involved with. I wanted to hear what he had to say about it."

Betty chose that moment to walk in with a tray of drinks. Jeremy had a dry martini and Cynthia took the Bloody Mary.

"Would you like something, sir?" she asked me, giving no indication that a few minutes ago her mistress and I had been sleeping buck-naked on the floor.

"I'll pass. It's a little early for me," I said.

Cynthia walked over to her husband and stood behind him, rubbing his neck. "I was riding by the Casillos and I saw Mr. Resnick on their porch. I thought he might be a buyer, but no such luck. When he told me he wanted some information about the Casillos, I asked him to come by. I was hoping you'd get home early."

"I'm sure," Jeremy said, smiling. "Was Cynthia able to help you?"

"We had just started talking when you arrived."

"I see."

You could read a million things into the way he said those two words.

"I understand they wound up in Mexico," I said quickly.

Jeremy nodded. "Yes, it was about three years ago, after the baseball season. I really wasn't very close to Augie. My wife was friends with Theresa and we had them over for dinner several times, and we were their guests. Then Theresa came down with cancer and she and Augie were having a bad time of it financially.

"Major-league umpires make very little money, maybe fifty or sixty thousand after twenty years. The hospital costs left him almost penniless. I know he borrowed from his friends and family, and one day he showed up here and asked for a substantial loan. Well, against my better judgment, but with my wife's urging, I lent him fifty thousand dollars. He used the money to take his wife to some experimental clinic in Mexico, and that's the last anyone saw of Augie and Theresa.

"Dear, we did get that letter from Augie . . ."

"Oh yes, Cynthia's right. There was a letter from Augie letting us know that Theresa had died. That was basically all the letter said."

"Did you ever make an attempt to recover your money?"

"Mr. Resnick, I'm an investment banker. I handle great sums of other people's money. The last thing in the world I'd like anyone to know is that I threw fifty thousand dollars into the sewer. I knew when I gave him the money that I probably would never be repaid."

"Why was that?"

"Well, what did he have here? His house was already mortgaged to the hilt. He was getting close to mandatory retirement in his job. He had no family here. If he came back to the States, he would have had to spend the rest of his life working to repay his debts. In Mexico, he was free to start over."

"If you knew all that, why did you lend him the money?"

"I asked him to," Cynthia said. "Sometimes you

have to think with your heart and not with your head. Augie felt it was Theresa's last chance. I couldn't say no to him."

"My wife has a lot of trouble saying no," Jeremy said evenly.

I pretended I didn't hear him.

"By any chance, do you have the name of this clinic?" I asked.

"I have the name somewhere," Cynthia said. "I think it's in the den."

"Would you have a picture of Augie? I can probably get one from the major-league office, but it would be very helpful if you had one."

"Give him the shot of the four of us that we took at Christmas," Jeremy said. "Are you thinking of finding him in Mexico, Mr. Resnick?"

"Possibly."

"Well, I wish you luck. I'll even give you a further incentive. You can have a third of whatever money you can recover for me."

Jeremy downed the rest of his martini in two quick gulps.

"Let me see if I can get those things for you," Cynthia said, moving away from Jeremy and leaving the room.

Her husband's eyes followed her out of the room. "She's a very beautiful woman, isn't she, Slots?"

"Very beautiful."

"She was a client of mine. That's how we met."

"You're a fortunate man, Mr. Marsh."

He stared into the bottom of his martini glass. "Yes, I guess I am," he murmured quietly.

Pause.

"Is there a Jeff Davis that figures into the case you're working on?"

"Why?"

"Before Augie left, he was almost paranoid about this Davis fellow coming after him. Perhaps that's another reason he didn't return to the States."

Cynthia came back carrying a manila envelope. "Here, I found it." She handed the envelope to me.

There was a printed brochure describing the benefits of *La Nueva Día Clínica* and its director, Dr. Milagros Rodriguez. The clinic used alternative therapies to the traditional ways of treating cancer, including a holistic diet, laetrile, and biofeedback. There was also a picture of the Marshes and the Casillos around a well-stocked table. Theresa Casillo was a plain-looking woman with straight hair and a sad little smile. Augie was heavyset, with a jolly round face over a slight double chin. He was waving at the camera with a turkey leg in one hand and a can of beer in the other. In the picture, Jeremy Marsh seemed to be looking at Augie's antics with distaste, while Cynthia seemed to be enjoying the umpire.

"Do you want these back?" I asked them.

"I'd like the picture back," Cynthia said.

"You see, my wife was a good friend of Theresa's," Jeremy said sarcastically.

What he was really saying was that he thought Cynthia had been playing around with Augie.

"Well, thank you both very much. Perhaps I get the chance to take you up on your offer, Mr. Marsh."

"I hope you do," Jeremy replied.

I told them not to bother walking me to the door, that I could find my way out myself.

"I have the greatest confidence in you," Jeremy Marsh said in that quiet, assured voice of his.

9

• • • • • • • • • • • • • • • •

t was late afternoon and the weather was turning
colder.

I parked in a bus stop and walked the two short
blocks to Capaldo's. There were a few stragglers left
from the lunch crowd and Frankie was in the rear
going over the additions on the waiters' checks. He
looked up at me and held his hand up so I wouldn't say
anything that would screw up his count.

Finally, he nodded his head. "Hey, Slots. How ya
doin'? You want something? You eat yet?"

"I'm fine, Frankie. Father Quinn in the back?"

"You kiddin' me? Every afternoon for twenty-two
years, waddaya think, today's any different? Go on
through, you know where he is."

Harry Quinn was on the phone jotting down numbers on a pad. "St. Johns plus six; Rutgers plus two;
and Syracuse plus one and a half. Okay, Sam, thanks."

"How's business, Father?"

"It always falls off after the football season. There'll
be a lull now until the baseball season. I take college
basketball solely as a courtesy to my clients.

"So tell me, Slots. Did you find anything at the Casillo house?"

I gave him a rundown of my meeting with the Marshes, leaving out the more intimate details.

Quinn leaned back in his chair and thought about it.

"You'll be wanting to trace Augie then."

I shrugged. "Up to you, Father. Are you sure you want me to continue with this?"

"Well, I'm thinking about the boy. He's certainly changed for the better since you started to look into this thing. I think we have to follow through."

"I'm thinking of the boy, too. Maybe the best thing to do is let Davis' guilt or innocence be a matter of opinion. It will probably end up that way anyhow. If I do track down Casillo, I doubt he's going to give us something new. Those that believe in Davis will continue to do so and those that don't won't. I don't mind soaking up some sun and filling up on burritos, but you're paying the freight, Harry."

"I promised the boy I'd see it through to the end. That was our deal, and I can't renege on it. I just wish we could have something to hang our hopes on."

Quinn tapped the table with his fingertips.

"Harry, how many baseball games have you seen in the last twenty years?"

"Good Lord, Slots. I don't know. Maybe a thousand. Why?"

"I was just thinking. When the ball's in play, you're watching where the ball goes. When the ball isn't in play, what do you watch?"

"You mean between innings? Well, I ... I guess that's the time to go to the john, or to get a hot dog."

"If you're at the game you might watch your favorite player, right?"

"Okay, Slots. What's your point?"

"What do the umpires do when the ball isn't in play?"

"Well, they ..."

"Do they go into the dugouts? Do they get together and talk? Do they switch positions? Do they stay put?"

Quinn thought about it. "I . . . I guess I never noticed."

"Sure. The only time anyone notices the umpires is when they're involved in a play."

"I think I'm getting your drift, Slots," Quinn said, nodding thoughtfully.

"Let's pretend that Davis was telling the truth originally, and he didn't pack his glove with Vaseline. Then the one who did it had to be Casillo."

"Sure! He had the stuff in his own pocket. He takes a gob of it in his palm, takes Jeff's glove and sticks it in there. But, Slots, there were sixty thousand people watching the game at the stadium, plus network TV."

"Come on, Harry. Magicians make elephants disappear on stage, and you're looking for the trick."

"Good Lord! I'll bet that's how it was done."

"Easy, Harry, this is just pretend, remember? There are three big hurdles. The first is to find Augie Casillo. The second is what would Augie's motive be? And the third is Davis' own confession that he actually is guilty as accused. Every one of them is a stumbling block."

"I bet you were one of those kids in kindergarten that waited until the other kids built skyscrapers with their blocks and then you'd come and knock them down." Harry sighed. "Well, I'll tell you, Slots. They've got this slogan for the New York State Lottery, 'You've got to be in it, to win it.'"

"Meaning?"

"Meaning, get your arse down to Mexico, my boy."

The Answerphone was blinking away, letting me know that someone had left a message. I hit the "play" button and Cynthia Marsh's voice came on.

"Slots, it's Cynthia. I got your number from the phone book. I hope you call in for your messages because I have to talk to you tonight. Please call me the moment you hear this. But don't call my house! I'm at a friend's place and it's very important that you call me here and not at my home. I don't want Jeremy to know I've called you. Please, Slots, it's very important!"

She gave me a 516 exchange phone number that I wrote down. Cynthia had sounded upset and frightened. I dialed the number and a woman answered.

"Cynthia Marsh, please."

"Yes, hold on . . ."

I heard a muffled sound as she called Cynthia to the phone.

"Slots, I'm so glad you called. I've got to talk to you."

"That's one of the advantages of a telephone."

"No, I mean I have to see you and talk to you. I can't say some things over the phone. Can you meet me tonight?"

I only had to pack a couple of shirts and some slacks, make flight reservations . . .

"Come to my office," I told her.

"No. Someplace else. He might have the office watched."

"Who?"

"Jeremy. I'll explain it all to you when I see you. Do you know where the Hard Rock Café is on Fifty-seventh?"

"Yes."

"Meet me there in an hour. Please, Slots, it's very important. There'll be a man at the door named Patrick. Tell him you're waiting for me."

She hung up.

It would take me twenty minutes to make it uptown and park in a lot. I finished packing and used my credit card to book a flight to Mexico City in the morning on Pan Am.

I had a little time to reflect on Cynthia Marsh as I nosed the Porsche up Third Avenue. I pegged her as a spoiled rich kid. Jeremy had said that she had been one of his clients, so I was right in my assumption that she'd started with money before she married him. The roll in the hay with me was as much a result of boredom as it was finding me attractive. I wondered if it gave her an extra boot knowing her husband might come home and find us.

Cynthia Marsh was as unpredictable as she was beautiful. She was looking for adventure, and that could spell big trouble.

The Hard Rock Café had become the mecca of the teenyboppers and yuppie sets. The building on Fifty-seventh Street had a kind of novel logo—a half of an automobile poking through the concrete. The car looked to be of the late-fifties or early-sixties vintage, a shined-up steel-and-chrome signature representing the time when rock 'n' roll moved out of its black Southern gospel roots and went mainstream.

The line in front of the place extended three-quarters of a block. A burly red-faced bouncer in a tuxedo kept everyone in the front behind a velvet rope. He would admit two or three people as two or three came out.

"I'm looking for Patrick," I told him.

"You found him. What's the beef?"

"I'm a friend of Cynthia Marsh."

"Ten feet behind me there's a little door. Walk in there fast and close it behind you *fast*. I've seen them try and storm their way in and it's ugly. There's a guy there named Eddie in a monkey suit. He'll take you to Miss Marsh."

I found the side door and walked in. Another bouncer in a tux stopped me after two steps.

"You have business here, pal?" he asked, on the edge of annoyance.

"Patrick told me to find Eddie. I'm Cynthia Marsh's friend."

He looked me over as if trying to figure out if I was lying. I must have passed inspection.

"Okay, I'll take you to her table. Let me dead-bolt the lock."

I followed him into the very crowded café and he led me past the bar and up to a balcony, where he motioned for me to take the corner table. There were clumps of loudspeakers hanging chandelier-like over each table, blasting out sounds that resembled music. I had to read Eddie's lips when he told me that Cynthia would be right back.

The café was in actuality a kind of museum dedicated to rock 'n' roll memorabilia. There were guitars, costumes, gold and platinum records, photographs, and dozens of other sacred mementos donated by the likes of Elvis, Lennon, Chuck Berry, et cetera, hung in places of honor on three walls. Another wall had symbols of the world's religions and represented a multimedia expression of peace and love.

Cynthia emerged from the bathroom. She caught my eye and waved. She was only wearing a pair of acid jeans and a man-tailored shirt, but she turned heads at every table she passed.

Part of the fun in going to a place like the Hard Rock Café was to spot celebrities. From the attention she was getting from the patrons, they obviously thought of her as a movie star or a high-fashion model.

She slid into the chair next to mine and leaned over to yell in my ear as she handed me rubber earplugs. "Take these! Otherwise you'll get a headache."

I plugged in the ear blockers and the decibel count from the speakers went down considerably.

"Can you hear me now?" she asked.

I nodded yes. "Why did you pick this place, for God's sake?"

"Safety precaution. No one can hear what we're saying, and if I was being followed, or you were, they would have to wait on line for two hours before they could get in."

She smiled at me. "How about a drink?"

"Scotch straight up," I told her.

She turned around to a waiter who was bringing coffee to another table and had him lip-read her order. She ordered a Scotch for herself also. He nodded and went off to the bar.

"What's going on?" I asked her.

"My husband is not what he seems," she said nervously. "He looks like a quiet, dignified pillar of the community, but that's not Jeremy at all. He's ruthless and he's dangerous. You can't imagine what lengths he'll go to to *get* something he wants, and what lengths he'll go to to *keep* something he owns."

"Does he own you?"

Her eyes flashed. "Yes, he owns me. I'm as much his possession as his cars or his jewelry."

"Why tell me?"

"I think he knows about us," she said.

The waiter came by and set down our drinks. Cynthia took a quick long swallow. She wasn't playacting, she was very scared.

"Thanks for the warning," I told her. "I'll look both ways before I cross the street."

She shook her head. "Please, Slots, don't brush it off. Jeremy is capable of anything . . . including murder."

Suddenly some loose ends clicked into place. "You think he killed Augie," I said, and watched as the blood drained from her face.

"How . . . how did you know that?"

"You could have warned me about your jealous husband on the phone, so I knew you had something else to tell me. I brought up the subject of Augie at the house and it was obvious from the way Jeremy talked that he felt you and Augie had something going on between you. Even the way you looked at his picture was a tip-off. Do you have any proof?"

"No, I just know that Augie wouldn't disappear without getting in touch with me. We had a . . . a . . . very intense relationship. It stopped after Theresa became ill. Augie and I both had a case of the guilts and we stopped seeing each other. I even persuaded Jeremy to lend Augie the money for Theresa's health care."

"You mean the clinic in Mexico?"

"Yes. There was nothing traditional medicine could do for her, so Augie was willing to try anything. He read about *Nueva Día* in some magazine and he came to me for the money. There was no way that I could get my hands on fifty thousand without Jeremy knowing about it, so I asked him to loan Augie the money."

"Why would he help Augie if he thought you two were having an affair?"

"Slots, listen to me. He's not like you or me. He never gives himself away. He's as cold and calculating as a machine. He's like a walking computer. He waits and watches and when you least expect it, he strikes. Maybe he wanted him out of the country. Maybe he felt it would be easier to kill him in Mexico."

"You're throwing around accusations. What makes you think Augie was killed? What if, after Theresa died, he continued to feel guilty about the affair? Why come back to the States and have to repay Jeremy?"

Cynthia shook her head. "Slots, the day after we got that letter from Augie saying Theresa died, I showed it to Jeremy. 'That's the last you'll ever hear of him,' he said. Then he looked at me with a look that to this day scares the hell out of me. Then he repeated, *'You'll never see him again, Cynthia.'* The way he said it, I know it meant that Augie was dead."

"Maybe."

"There would be no other reason in the world for Augie not to get in touch with me. We loved each other."

She sipped some more of her Scotch and used her napkin to wipe away a big tear that had welled up.

"I want you to find out what happened to Augie," she told me. "I want to hire you . . ."

"I'm already on the case. I leave for Mexico tomorrow morning. Do you feel you're in any danger?"

She laughed. "I'm his pet, like a show dog or a thoroughbred. He likes to have me around to parade in front of company, to give him an air of respectability. So far, I haven't outlived my usefulness."

"Is Jeremy a homosexual?"

"As far as I can see, he's asexual. He's in love with power and money."

"Leave him."

"I can't."

"Are you afraid of him?"

"There are things I can't tell you . . . I can't leave him."

She had been watching the entranceway as she was talking to me. Suddenly, she stiffened. "Oh, God!"

"What's the matter?"

I followed her gaze to a white-haired man wearing a beige trench coat, who was standing near the doorway looking around the room.

"Who is he?" I asked her.

"He must work for Jeremy. I think he's following me. He shouldn't see us together."

She got up. "Go to Mexico and find out what happened to Augie. Somebody has to stop Jeremy. Go now and don't let him see you!"

She walked away from me and back toward the bathroom. I watched as the white-haired man saw her and followed her with his eyes. He stationed himself near the bar and waited for her to come out of the bathroom. When she did, he picked up a menu and hid his face so she wouldn't see him.

Cynthia played her role out, talking to some people at one of the tables and pretending she didn't see the guy who was tailing her.

I picked up the glass with her Scotch and carefully spilled out what was left into my glass. Then I wrapped hers with a napkin and hoped I wouldn't smudge the prints.

When I made it back into the street, I thought the

blaring music had made me deaf until I realized I still had the earplugs in.

I retrieved the Porsche after paying the ransom they charged in the parking garage, and made a stop at the Manhattan North Precinct. One of the detectives there whom I had personally promoted was a gentle giant of a man with an unpronounceable Polish last name that had been shortened to Stash.

Stash gave me a warm greeting and we shared some gossip and talked about the old days. I asked him to do me a favor and try to get Forensics to lift some prints from Cynthia Marsh's glass and run them through Records.

"What are you lookin' for, Chief?" Stash asked.

"I don't know. It's a fishing expedition. There's also a guy I need checked out." I wrote down "Jeremy Marsh" and his address. "That's Cynthia's husband."

"Can you give me a couple of days?"

"Take your time. I'm on my way to Mexico in the morning."

"Vacation?"

"No, it's a case."

I thanked Stash and made my way back to the convertible sofa in my office. Before I fell asleep, I thought about Cynthia and Jeremy.

Question after question went through my mind. What had happened to Augie? What did Jeremy have as a hold over his wife? Just where and how did Jeff Davis fit in? Lots of questions . . . and very few answers.

10

● ● ● ● ● ● ● ● ● ● ● ● ● ● ● ●

I'm not wild about flying. Most people, if they are really honest with themselves, feel the same way. The airlines know this and that's why they're constantly sending stewardesses up and down the aisles with food, drink, magazines, blankets, and anything else they can think of to get your mind off the fact that the only thing separating you from belly-whopping into the ground is a couple inches of steel.

It took six hours until the plane landed at Benito Juarez International Airport in Mexico City. A salesman from Omaha spent four of those hours trying to convince me how important it was for me to purchase life insurance. First there was the guy on the phone, and now a guy on the plane pushing term insurance. If I were superstitious, which I'm not (knock wood), I might have figured it was some kind of omen. As it was, I finally had to give the guy the brush-off because he was interfering with my concentration, which I'm sure was the only thing keeping the Pan Am jet in the air.

I had no idea what time it was in Mexico City. All I could tell upon disembarking was that it was still daylight and the airport thermometer read 91 degrees. Next to the thermometer was an ad for Miller beer, and a sign that said: "Low this month 46 degrees. High 70 degrees." I arrive and the place turns into a blast furnace.

I got mobbed by three wiry cabdrivers dressed in oversized Hawaiian shirts, jeans, and sandals. Each of them tried to line me up as a fare.

"I speak English," one of them said.

I pointed to him. "Okay, pal, you're hired."

The other two guys ran after the next passenger.

I found myself yawning, keeping a jet aloft always knocks me out.

"I need to take a nap, pal. Take me to the nearest hotel."

He nodded his head and pulled my arm for me to follow him until we got to his cab. I suppose there were more horrible-looking cars on the road, but I had never seen any. At one time, it might have been an old Chevy Impala, but now it was an amalgam of parts from a dozen different cars, welded together by a madman. There were three sets of fenders, a fin from a Plymouth Belvedere on the roof making the vehicle look like Jaws, two different-colored and different-sized bumpers, doors from a Volkswagen Beetle, which didn't fit on the car's frame but were attached anyway, and a rear trunk that looked like an icebox. Those were the parts I could recognize.

"What the hell do you call this?" I asked him.

The man, who was short, walnut brown, and completely bald, said, "I speak English."

"Yeah, I know. That's why I hired you. Just take me to the nearest hotel."

He looked at me and smiled a big gap-toothed smile and said, "I speak English."

"I guess you do," I muttered. I mimed closing my

eyes and going to sleep. "Hacienda . . . hotel . . ." I told him.

"I speak English," he said, but got the cab going after the engine coughed and sputtered a half dozen times.

The eight-mile trip from the airport might have been worth the three hundred pesos I gave my taxi-driving friend, but I wouldn't know. I was asleep as soon as we hit the highway. I remember seeing the Golden Arches of McDonald's and the comforting feeling of home "over three billion served" gave me.

The next thing I remember was Mr. I Speak English shaking me awake in front of a nice-looking hotel called El Presidente. I paid the driver and checked into the modern building. An eighty-year-old "boy" took my baggage to a fourth-floor room that looked like every other hotel room in the world, and without taking off my clothes, I fell on the bed and went right to sleep.

It was the next morning when I shook myself out of bed. I showered, shaved, slapped on a dash of cologne, and I was ready to get to work.

This time I asked the desk clerk to get me an English-speaking taxi driver.

"You can rent a car for yourself with a driver for maybe twenty American dollars. If you want an English-speaking driver, it is double."

"That sounds okay."

"Then you have to pay for the gas."

"Fair enough."

"Then there is the fee of ten American dollars for me to get you this service."

"Of course," I said.

"Then, no problem. I will get you the best," he assured me.

I waited in the lobby for "the best" to arrive. He turned out to be a chubby black man wearing a Mickey

Mouse T-shirt, straw Panama, black pants, and sandals.

"Lookin' for a driver?" he asked.

"You're not Mexican."

"You ain't no Eskimo, but I don't hold it against you. My man Rivera says you need a driver. Well, here I is." He did a little two-step and finished off with his arms outstretched.

"You know your way around?" I asked.

"Fifteen years souff o' de bowdah. I take you anywhere yor li'l ole heart desires."

I pulled out the paper Cynthia had given me with the name of the clinic and its address. "Can you take me there?"

The black man's mood turned somber. "Yup, I know the place. It's about halfway between here and Cuernavaca. It's a couple, maybe three hours' ride."

"You got a name?"

"They call me Bambi."

"Well, how about getting started?"

"Follow me, sir," he said.

At least Bambi's car was recognizable. It was a four-year-old Oldsmobile that shone like a newly minted penny. The inside was just as clean.

"I'm impressed," I told him.

"My daddy always told me to take care of the tools you make your livin' with. What's your name?"

"Slots. Slots Resnick."

"Okay, Mr. Slots Resnick, I got me a full tank of gas, so you replace what we use."

"Fine."

We pulled away from the curb and immediately got stuck in a traffic jam. It was still early in the morning, and it felt as hot as it did yesterday.

"Bambi, you have air-conditioning in this limo?"

"Yeah, but I gots to charge you extra."

"Okay, but just charge me for what *I* use, and you stay warm."

He thought that was funny, so he repeated it to himself and laughed again.

"Say, Mr. Slots Resnick, it ain't none of my business, but man, you don't look like you is sick."

"I'm not. I've got to go to the clinic to ask about a friend."

That seemed to brighten Bambi's mood considerably. "Well, that's okay then. I don't like carryin' no real sick people aroun'. I don't care what they say, man. All that cancer shit is catching."

We lurched forward as traffic started to move again. I asked him about Augie and drew a blank.

"I ain't much of a baseball fan. But man, I do love that jai alai! You got games every night but Monday and Friday. A man can make some serious money bettin' at the fronton. Hey, Slots Resnick, you ever been to Meheeco befo'?"

"First trip."

"Man, if you want some terrific buys, I'll take you to the Niza. You can pick up some great silver, and leather, all kinds of handcrafted shit. And these peasants, man, they is a pushover for a man from the States, 'specially if he got the big Bambi at his side. You got blankets, pottery, onyx, tin, copper . . ."

"Not this trip."

"Maybe you like the company of the señoritas? Old Bambi fix you up real good."

"I don't think I'll be here that long, amigo."

"Well, man, I get you anything . . . 'cept guns. Them Federales are fuckin' out of their minds when they catch you with a damn gun."

I didn't have my gun with me. I had left it back in the office. I would have had to get permission from the airlines and then permission from the Mexican government to carry it. It wasn't worth the hassle.

Bambi liked to talk and it didn't matter if I answered him or not. He just kept on going. I learned more than I wanted to know about his life. He was a country boy

111

from Georgia who got stationed in Texas when he was in the army. On a three-day pass, he got bombed in Tijuana and woke up married to a Mexican girl. It was a scam to extort money from the gringo soldiers, but he fell in love with the girl and she with him. They settled in Mexico City, where he and his Carmen had three kids, a dog, two cats, and a half dozen chickens.

I interrupted the biography of Bambi and asked him if we could find a place to stop and eat. We were about an hour away from the hotel and my stomach was still on Eastern Standard Time.

"You see, Slots Resnick, in Mexico lunch is the heavy meal. They pack it away until maybe four-thirty, five o'clock. Supper begins at nine P.M. Lucky for you, old Bambi has some friends in this neck of the woods."

We rode another ten minutes and Bambi pulled the Olds off the highway and onto an unpaved back road. After five more minutes of rocking and rolling, we stopped at a small farm.

"Be right back," Bambi said, walking toward the farmhouse.

He emerged a few minutes later carrying a plate and planting a big kiss on the lips of a heavyset Mexican woman, who laughed shyly at what Bambi was telling her.

"Here you go, my man," he said, passing the plate to me. "You got pineapple, pomegranates, guavas, mangoes, and zapote. That's good for your stomach."

We started up again as I tried the fruit.

"Thanks, it's delicious."

"Don't worry, I'm gonna charge you for it."

La Nueva Día Clínica looked more like a resort than a medical facility. It sprawled out over several acres, with beautiful glass-and-stone ranch-style buildings, all air-conditioned and modern.

We passed an exercise building, a large cafeteria, a building called the Rehab Center, the Meditation

Building, the X-Ray Lab, and the Intergroup Facility.
All the buildings had their names written in English.

"Most of the clients are from the States," Bambi
said, reading my mind.

We rode on a fine gravel road around the three buildings that were called Energizing Centers and then
came to the Administration building.

A man dressed in a white smock waved for us to
stop. "Hi, there, I'm Dr. Nardone. May I be of service?"
he said, leaning on the car and looking in the window.

"I'm Mr. Resnick; I would like to talk to someone
about the clinic and—"

"Yes, of course," he said, shaking his head, "I understand. If you'd like to park right here, I'll take you to
our director, Dr. Rodriguez."

He obviously thought I was very sick. He should
have seen me before I shaved. If it was going to get me
an interview with the head honcho, I wasn't going to
correct him.

He looked at Bambi. "If you'd like, sir, you can have
something in our cafeteria."

"I stay right here. Thank you jes' the same."

I remembered Bambi's theory about catching dis-
eases.

"Won't you follow me, sir?" he said.

I got out of the car and followed Nardone into the
Administration Building. Two people who looked like
patients passed us along the way.

"It's a glorious day," the first one said, smiling.

"A glorious day!" Dr. Nardone agreed.

"I'm getting better every minute," an elderly lady
with a walker told the doctor.

"Every minute of every day, we're getting stronger in
every way," he rhymed.

A secretary gave Nardone a cheery greeting and he
responded likewise.

"I see everybody's upbeat around here."

"Yes, that's the secret of *Nueva Día*. How much do you know about us?"

I pulled out the brochure I had in my pocket.

"Oh, yes. That's a bit outdated, but I'll let Dr. Rodriguez explain our program to you."

We came to a door with DR. MILAGROS RODRIGUEZ, DIRECTOR, on the nameplate. Nardone tapped twice and a voice called out, "Come in, please."

"It's a brand-new, wonderful day, and we have someone here interested in the clinic," Nardone said.

"Every day is a wonderful day, Doctor. Thank you so much for bringing the gentleman here."

Nardone turned to me and backed out the door. "Have a wonderful day," he said with that great Cheshire-cat smile.

"I wish you everything you wish me, in spades," I said, getting into the swing of things.

Dr. Milagros Rodriguez was a dark-haired, dark-eyed Mexican beauty wearing a white smock identical to the one Dr. Nardone was wearing. Her figure was hidden by the shapeless garment, but I was willing to bet she had a knockout of a body.

She held out her hand for me to shake, and guess what? She was smiling.

"I know, I know. We seem very strange to you, Mr. Mr. . . ?"

"Resnick."

"I sometimes forget how different we are on first greeting. I have to remind myself that to a newcomer we might seem a little weird."

She spoke with the slightest of accents, a little slurring of the "r."

"It's kind of different," I admitted.

She clasped her hands together. "Please sit down." She sat back behind the desk, with me across from her.

The room was painted white, with bright fluorescents. I sat in a comfortable leather chair.

"You see, we think—and there are many studies that

bear this out—actually, we are convinced that the cause of disease is emotional instability. When a person loses a job, or a loved one, or some other tragedy occurs, the forces within the body, the immune systems, break down. Here, at Nueva Día, we are constantly working to achieve harmony with our systems. We do this by enjoying life, by smiling, by laughter. We eat foods that are filled with the joy of life. Fruits and vegetables that have soaked up the sunshine and are rich in life-giving nutrients."

"No meat?"

"No flesh of dead animals. It is totally contrary to the laws of nature," she said. Smiling.

I knew a couple of lions that would disagree with her, but I kept my mouth shut.

"I noticed the names of some of the buildings. The Energizer Building, the Intergroup Building . . ."

"Yes, the Energizing Center is where our guests recharge their bodies. You might call it sleep, but here we say energize because even in the sleeping phase our guests are given subliminal messages that make them stronger every day."

"In every way," I added.

Dr. Rodriguez smiled approvingly.

"The Intergroup Building?"

"That is where the patients compare their progress. You also saw the Biofeedback Center, where we train our bodies and minds to fight disease and rid ourselves of the body's enemies."

"So you cure cancer?"

"Oh, yes. I myself have had cancer three times. I am now completely cured. There is not a trace of it in my body. We have hundreds of stories of tumors, some as large as grapefruits, completely disappearing."

"That sounds great."

"It is great, Mr. Resnick."

She looked at me and touched my hand. "What problem are you afflicted with?"

"Dr. Rodriguez, I hope I don't break this very warm spirit that I feel from you, but I'm not here for myself as a patient."

She looked surprised. "A loved one then?"

"No, you see, I'm an investigator from New York City. I'm trying to track down the husband of a former patient."

I expected to see a change in her attitude, but she surprised me.

"I'm so happy that you are not with disease. Of course, we will do everything within our power to help you. I don't mind talking about our clinic, Mr. Resnick. Restating our goals and philosophy is just as important for me as it is for any of our guests."

"Do you mind if I ask you another question?"

"Please."

"How much does a stay at Nueva Día cost?"

"It's expensive, but equal in price to some American traditional hospitals. Almost a thousand dollars a day."

I nodded. "I guess you get what you pay for."

"I only wish we could treat everyone for nothing. But we digress. Please tell me whom you are seeking?"

"The guest's name was Theresa Casillo. She passed away here three years ago."

"Sometimes they come when it is too late and the process cannot be reversed."

"Her husband was with her. He's the fellow I'm interested in finding. His name is Augie Casillo. Do husbands and wives stay in the Energizing Center together?"

"Of course. They can be a great help for the afflicted. Mr. Resnick, if you will stay here a moment or so, I will personally look into the files. Three years?"

"Yes."

She walked out the door and closed it behind her. I checked the medical degrees she had behind her desk. She had been an undergrad at Columbia, and worked for her doctorate in a college I'd never heard of. Her doctorate was in Nutrition.

I was in my chair by the time she came back. She had a manila folder in her hand. The name T. CASILLO was handwritten in red ink on the cover.

"Yes, I have her file here. Let's see, she was a guest for five weeks before she passed on."

Five weeks was thirty-five days, at a thousand bucks a day, times two because of Augie. That meant seventy grand!

"Yes, her case was too advanced. If she had only come to us sooner . . ." Dr. Rodriguez shook her head.

"Do you have anything about her husband?"

"Just that he asked us to cremate the body and, oh yes, here's his address."

I walked behind her and looked over her shoulder. It was the address of his Connecticut home.

"I have that. May I take a look?"

She handed the files to me and I thumbed through them. There were pages of medical mumbo jumbo, and biofeedback mumbo jumbo, and diets, and shots of vitamins, and a slew of other things, but not a word about Augie.

"Do you think there might be some staff member who would remember the couple?"

"I doubt it, but let's try."

She made a few phone calls and spoke to the three staff members whose names were on the files. For the most part, they remembered Theresa as a small, sad woman who had come too late for the clinic to help her. One of them recalled that her husband had been in baseball in some capacity. Other than that, it was a blank.

I read the dates of Theresa's stay at the clinic. She had arrived on the first of November and died on December 6. It looked as if Augie had disappeared from earth on that same day.

I thanked Dr. Rodriguez and hid my disappointment

with a cheery smile. I promised I would spread the word about the clinic's good work to my fellow New Yorkers, even though I knew few people who could foot the bill.

"Isn't there a bill for Theresa's and Augie's stay?"

"Oh yes. That would be in our accounting office."

"Would you mind if . . ."

"Not at all. Just ask Laura in Accounting. She's across the hall and she'll be happy to help you."

Dr. Rodriguez got up and shook my hand. We both beamed smiles at each other.

Laura in Accounting proved to be just as accommodating as everyone else at the Happy Farm. I gave her the dates of Theresa's and Augie's stay and she punched it into her computer terminal. In a second the screen filled up with columns of "Services" and "Payments." I told her to skip to December 6, the day Theresa died.

I didn't see anything I could use until the very last page.

"What are those numbers?" I asked, trying to contain my excitement.

"Oh, we have a switchboard. When guests make a call, we have to charge them for it. We just can't absorb the expense."

I was looking at the last four numbers. Two were local calls and two were calls to the States.

"May I have a copy of that page?" I asked her.

"My pleasure, sir."

She pushed another button and a laser printer came up with a copy in two seconds.

"Thanks. You people are great!" I said.

"We get stronger and stronger every day," she told me, smiling.

Bambi had the engine running and he was waiting for me near the door of the Administration Building.

"You find what you was lookin' fo'?" he wanted to know.

"I'm not sure. Would you mind if I rode up in the front with you?" I asked him. "I'm uncomfortable with this chauffeur stuff."

"Sho' you wanta mix wiff the common folk?" Bambi said. "C'mon then."

I sat next to him and looked over the paper I took from the clinic. The two calls to the States had area codes I recognized. One was Connecticut, the other was Jersey. The calls were made in rapid succession. The computer listed the times for each. First came the local call to Mexico City, then the call to Jersey, then the call to Connecticut, and finally the call to Mexico City.

"What the hell!" Bambi yelled.

He was staring at a car in his rearview mirror. The driver had come from out of nowhere and was trying to pass.

"I ain't goin' fast enuf fo' you? Well, less see you keep up now," Bambi said.

I didn't like the look of this. It didn't appear to be the typical game of "chicken" where Mexicans proved their machismo.

He floored the Oldsmobile and pulled away from the car behind. It was a Lincoln Town Car and the driver wasn't giving up. He got behind Bambi and rammed him hard. The sun was glaring off the Lincoln's windshield, stopping me from seeing who the driver was.

I made a reflexive grab for my gun, then realized it was in a locked drawer in New York.

"I kill that motha!" Bambi swore.

The Lincoln smashed into us again, jolting me back into the seat.

"What you want, man?" Bambi yelled.

Bambi's speedometer registered eighty and the Lincoln was still on our tail.

There was an open field to our right, off the shoulder of the road.

"Hang a sharp right, Bambi, and let him go by," I said.

The black man cut the wheel and we careened over the incline of the road and onto the dirt field.

The Lincoln rode right past us and continued on down the road. Then he swerved off the road and came after us.

"The man is nuts!" Bambi said.

He turned the car in a circle and the Lincoln followed us around. Now I got a look inside through the open window. I had only a quick glance at him but it was instant recognition. It was the white-haired man who had followed Cynthia into the Hard Rock Café.

"Hey, man, stop yo' playin'," Bambi called out as the Town Car drew alongside of us.

Bambi was looking at the man in the Lincoln and we were heading toward a group of trees.

"Bambi! Watch out!" I yelled.

He saw the trees and tried to brake.

Out of the corner of my eye I saw the man in the Lincoln pick something up from the seat of the car. His eyes met mine as he leveled the sawed-off shotgun out the window and pulled the trigger.

He had a clear shot at me, but Bambi jammed on the brakes to avoid the trees. The decelerating speed pushed him forward and the twelve-gauge blew off the door of the Olds and turned Bambi into a fountain of blood, his lifeless body jolting into mine with such force that it pushed me up against the passenger door.

The car was still moving at high speed and I threw Bambi off me and grabbed for the steering wheel. Another tree loomed up and I wasn't going to be able to stop. Bambi was lying across the seat, preventing me from moving my legs to get at the brake.

I pulled myself away from him and dived out of the passenger door a moment before the car crashed into the tree, spun, and flipped over. I landed in the soft grass and miraculously I felt okay. Everything seemed to be in one piece.

I turned just in time to see the Lincoln turn. He

gunned the car toward me. I had almost no time to react, but I managed to dive out of the way. The wheels missed me by scant inches.

I thought he would turn around and try again, but I was wrong. The Lincoln screeched to a dead stop and the man walked out of the car. He walked toward me cradling the sawed-off twelve-gauge in the crook of his arm. I watched him load the gun as he stood ten feet away from me.

"Big-shot detective," he sneered, aiming the gun at my chest.

There were two shots; one came from a distance, the other from the twelve-gauge. The first one chipped off a fistlike chunk from the killer's head, the second was caused by the spasmodic reflex of death. The twelve-gauge had fired harmlessly into the ground.

"Policía! Policía! No mueve, no mueve!"

Two men came running across the field. The taller of the two carried the rifle that had killed the man with the white hair.

They were an Abbott-and-Costello pair: a short fat man and a tall lean one.

I kept my hands in the air as they approached. They were jabbering at me in Spanish.

"Unless one of you guys speaks English, we've got a problem here," I said.

"Americano?" the fat guy asked.

"Yeah."

"Are you hurt?" he asked me brusquely.

"I don't think so. Can I put my hands down?"

"Yes, yes. of course."

He looked at his partner, who was going through the dead man's clothes.

"Qué?"

"Nada."

The fat guy looked at me. "The man has no identification or labels in his clothes. I am not surprised. Have you ever seen him before?"

If I said yes, I'd be spending the next three weeks in Mexico while they tried to figure out an angle.

"No. He just came up from behind and tried to kill us," I said.

"It's a lucky thing we were following you, señor."

I nodded. "It's just too bad you didn't get here a little sooner." I was looking down at Bambi's body.

"Don't waste any sympathy on him. He is the reason we were following you. This man is a very dangerous hombre. We suspect him in the killing of three American tourists. That is why we have followed you since leaving Mexico City," Costello said. "You have some papers of identity?"

I handed over my tourist card, which he looked over very carefully.

"You are Mr. Resnick, sí?"

"Yes."

"Bueno. I am Lieutenant Maldonato, and this is my partner, Señor Luis Reyes."

We shook hands formally and the three of us stared down at the bodies.

"This is simply a falling-out among thieves, señor," Maldonato explained. "I hope you do not get the wrong idea. Mexico is a very safe place generally. May I ask the nature of your visit?"

"I was inquiring about the Nueva Día Clinic."

"Say no more, Señor Resnick, I understand," Maldonato said solemnly.

He conversed with Reyes in Spanish for a couple of minutes and mentioned the clinic. Reyes looked at me and shrugged sadly.

"We will question Rivera at the hotel about this other man. Rivera would steer the tourists, and this Bambi would rob and kill them."

"He seemed like a nice guy," I said.

"Not to the practiced eye of one in law enforcement," Maldonato said smugly and patted me on the shoulder. "Ahh, but you, my friend, have other worries.

We will take you back to police headquarters in the city and we will ask you for a statement. I hope this will not inconvenience you too much. What is your occupation, señor?"

"I sell life insurance," I told him.

Maldonato nodded. "It is a noble business, protecting the loved ones who must carry on."

"He told me he was married with children," I said, looking down at Bambi.

Maldonato poked at the body with his toe. "This scum? No! He is only out of prison for three months, and not so coincidentally, two American schoolteachers and a businessman like yourself have vanished after checking into the hotel. But do not concern yourself with this business. It was obviously an assassination of Señor Bambi, and then he wished to kill you to be sure there were no witnesses."

The ride back to Mexico City seemed to take much less time than the ride coming out. I wondered if Bambi really had been going to try something with me? Before we left the field, Maldonato searched the Oldsmobile and found a pistol hidden under the spare tire in the trunk. What would be Bambi's MO? Pretend some trouble with the car, drive off the road, pull out the pistol and . . .

My thoughts also turned to the white-haired man. I knew that Bambi hadn't been the intended victim. The assassin had followed me out of New York and had probably been waiting at the clinic for me to arrive. Why?

For the moment it would seem that Cynthia's warning about Jeremy was well founded. He had killed Augie and I might be getting too close to the truth. Hold it, Slots. Back up and go slow. It was too easy to jump to conclusions. It was too easy to accept hypothesis as fact.

The cops at headquarters in Mexico City were as efficient as cops everywhere else in the world. What should have taken an hour stretched into three. Added to the Mexican situation were the Federales, Mexican soldiers who also doubled as street guards.

I finally completed my statement and Maldonato thanked me for my cooperation. I told it exactly as it happened, leaving out that I had seen the white-haired man before.

I was sitting in Maldonato's office, more like a cubicle really, and he shook my hand and said I could leave.

"Lieutenant, may I ask a favor of you?"

"Sí, Señor Resnick."

I moved my chair up close to his. "It is obvious that you are a man of the world, and not a stranger to the affairs of the heart."

Maldonato winked knowingly.

"I am looking for a woman who means a great deal to me."

Maldonato nodded. "I understand."

"I have no way to contact her. All I have are some phone numbers that I found among her things. Perhaps as a Detective Lieutenant you might suggest a way for me to find out about the numbers?"

"What you need, Señor Resnick, is a reverse phone book. One that is listed by number rather than one that is listed by the party's name."

"Exactly. Would you be able to find such a book?"

"We have many resources here in Mexico. I'm sure I could locate such a book right in this headquarters. The problem, señor, is that we are only allowed access to these books if we are working on a case which would require it."

I reached into my wallet and fished out a fifty-dollar bill.

Maldonato eyed Ulysses Grant. "Perhaps I could take a fast look. What harm would it do?"

He made no attempt to take the money. "How many numbers are we talking about?"

"Two. Two local Mexico City numbers."

"Hmmm, that would mean twice the risk."

I placed another fifty beside the first one. I put them down on the desk in front of the lieutenant. He picked up a piece of paper and covered the bills.

"Write the numbers here," he instructed me.

I put the two local numbers down from memory on the paper. He picked up the paper and with it the hundred smackers.

"Please wait here, Señor Resnick, and I will see if I can help you."

He came back a quarter of an hour later. He shrugged his shoulders. "Not too much luck, I'm afraid."

"Why?"

"The first number is for a local taxi company, the second number is for the airport. It is the reservation desk for Pan American. It would seem that your lady friend was making plans to leave Mexico."

I thanked Maldonato and left the station house.

Three years ago, almost to the day, on December 6, Theresa Casillo had died. Augie immediately called a taxi service to pick him up from the clinic and made reservations to go back home. In between that time he made two calls to the States, one to Newark and one to Connecticut.

There was nothing left for me to do in Mexico City. I went back to the hotel room, packed my things, and headed for the airport.

Mr. Rivera, the desk manager, was conspicuously absent.

• • • • • • • • • • • • • • • • • •

11

Grit, graffiti, cold, and vandalism, it was good to be back in the Apple. I pulled a five-hour jet-lag number this time, and when I woke up in my own bed, I felt that all was right with the world.

The Connecticut number belonged to Jeremy and Cynthia Marsh. No surprise there.

The Newark number had been disconnected. There was no record of it. I remembered that Jefferson Davis had been born and bred in Newark. Coincidence?

I gave Ducky a call at the league office and asked him to run a check for me. Sure enough, three years ago, Davis had listed the Newark number on his pension form.

Now what did I have?

Augie Casillo spends five weeks with his ailing wife in Mexico . . . spends over seventy grand, most of it Marsh's money . . . cremates his wife immediately when she dies . . . calls Davis and Marsh, in that order . . . and then presumably makes reservations to leave the country. End of the trail of Augie Casillo.

I phoned Stash and paced the floor for ten minutes, until someone picked up the phone and called him.

"Sorry, Chief," he said, "we were in the middle of an interrogation and I thought this lying pimp bastard was going to crack. We found two of his girls beaten badly in front of the son of a bitch's condo."

"No problem. Any luck with those prints?"

"Yes and no. It's a mixed bag. Let's talk."

I understood that Stash was leery of Internal Affairs' wiretaps. Everybody else in the world had rights, except cops.

"When's a good time? I owe you lunch."

"Make it at twelve at John's," he said.

"You got it."

My next call was the hardest one to make, but I saw no way out of it. Morris Ackerman was the mayoral aide assigned to act as the liaison between the Police Department and City Hall. Every city agency had someone, and we were stuck with Ackerman. The bad blood between us had started the moment I was assigned the job of Chief of Detectives.

It had been Morris' contention that I never gave the Mayor enough credit when we made a significant bust. Morris always wanted me to tell the press that the collar couldn't have been accomplished if the Mayor hadn't added extra personnel to the case, or that the Mayor's special hot-line number or task force had been the key to solving the crime.

I had this terrible habit in Morris' eyes of giving credit to the men in the field who'd actually busted their asses to get the job done.

It was my feeling, although I had nothing more than instinct to go by, that it was Morris Ackerman who had urged the new Commissioner Vargas to get rid of me, or make my job so untenable that I'd leave, which was exactly what I did. Now I had to call Morris for a favor.

I took a deep breath and dialed his number. Two different secretaries got on to pump me about what my call was in reference to before the great man himself got on the phone. I could picture him in his tweed sports jacket with the leather patches on the elbows, filling his pipe with Sail, and cradling the phone between his neck and shoulder.

"Slots, old man, you're the last person in the world I'd expect a call from," he said.

"I need a favor, Morris."

"Really?"

I could picture that balding ferret face puffing his pipe with smug satisfaction.

"Always ready to help an old pal. Tell me what you need, Slots."

"I'm working on a case and I'm stuck. I need somebody with juice to get some information for me." I tried to inject just the right amount of desperation in my voice.

"What kind of case are we talking about here?"

"Nothing heavy, just a run-of-the-mill—"

"Slots," he interrupted, "if you want me to help, you're going to have to give it to me straight," Morris said sternly.

"Okay," I sighed. "I've got a client that loaned a guy some money. He wants to get that money back, but the guy cut out to Mexico and I'm trying to get a line on him."

"Slots, let me get this straight. Are you telling me you're in the collection business now?"

"Well, it's just until I . . ."

"My God, man. I can't believe what I'm hearing. Slots Resnick chasing deadbeats?"

He was really enjoying this.

"I have clients, it's just until something comes along . . ."

"Sure, Slots, sure. It's too bad you couldn't fit in with the department. Well, one makes one's choices and has to live by them, I guess."

I counted to ten and forced myself to say, "Can you help me, Morris? It's kind of important to me."

"Sure, Slots, what are old friends for?" He dripped with sarcasm.

I told him I needed him to call a honcho at Pan Am to search through the Mexico City Pan Am computer three years ago, December sixth or seventh, and see if there had been a reservation made for New York by an Augie Casillo.

"I suppose I could get this info for you, Slots. You know I find it hard to believe that you're reduced to this."

He was rubbing my nose in it.

"Will you help me, Morris?"

"Sure, for old times' sake. Just remember, you owe me," he said.

I thanked him profusely and decided that I was adding another hundred to Harry Quinn's tab for that call.

John's Bar was what is known in the trade as a blue-collar bar. Most of the patrons were workingmen from the area who would come by during the day on their lunch hour or after work. Most of the guys would be wearing the uniform of a local elevator-repair company, or of a plumbing outfit.

Although John's was short on ambience, John Ramirez was the bartender/owner and he made up for that defect by serving unwatered booze and good conversation.

John himself had been a detective. When a bullet in the chest took him out of the lineup, he and his wife, Mary, purchased the bar from Loan Shark Frankie "the Gyp" Ryan, who'd wound up with a lucrative real estate business after serving a stretch at Attica.

I bellied up to the long oak bar and swapped small talk with John. He was much heavier now, with a swarthy face set on a bull neck. I waved off the beer he offered me and took a Scotch straight up.

When Stash walked in he greeted John, picked up a bottle of Heineken, and we walked to a quiet table in the back.

"Did you ever hear of the sun, Slots? That's that big orange blob in the sky. They say it shines in Mexico. Shit, man, you're as pasty-faced as ever!"

"I told you, my man, I'm all business. How does it look if a client sees me decked out in a suntan on his money? Sooo, what do we have?"

"Like I said, it's a mixed bag. Jeremy Marsh is a majordomo in two or three corporations. He's into venture capital, which means if you've got an idea, he puts up the cash to back you, except he doesn't do it for individuals, only big businesses."

"His own money?"

"No way! These guys never put up their own dough. He heads a group of ten or twelve millionaires in a company called Marsh Associates. He makes the decisions. He's supposed to be a genius, but a real son of a bitch."

"What else?"

"That's it. He's clean as a whistle."

"Tell me about Cynthia."

Stash shook his head. "Weird chick. Her old man was Bruce K. Orolenko, an immigrant watchmaker from Russia who started the Orolenko Watch Company, which you and I never heard of because the going price for an Orolenko watch starts at twenty-five thousand. The old man dies and leaves his fortune to his only heir, Cynthia. So I hear this and I figure rich boy meets rich girl—end of story. Then I run your fingerprints through Records and I can't believe my eyes. The girl has a rap sheet, priors the length of my arm."

"What kind of priors?"

"Name it. Prostitution, burglary, selling heroin, indecent exposure, fencing diamonds, arms selling . . . I can't believe it. She's not even thirty."

I finished what was left in my glass and signaled John to bring over another.

"You're sure we're talking about the same girl?"

"Same girl . . . Cynthia Marsh."

"You're talking about a couple of hard-time offenses."

"Nope. She beats the slammer almost every time. She served maybe six months in all. Big-time lawyers, pretty girl, big money behind her . . . she walks on a psycho. They send her to Bellevue for tests, she walks out a couple of months later. When she doesn't claim psycho, her lawyers get her off as an alcoholic, which she is. She put in a year at Smithers."

John brought over a refill for me and another beer for Stash.

"What do you make of a kid like this, Slots? She got everything handed to her and she still fucks it up."

"What's your last arrest date on her?"

"Nothing on her for the last couple of years. Maybe she straightened out."

"She couldn't be that straightened out. The glass I gave you to run through for prints had Scotch in it. The people at Smithers would be very disappointed."

"You know what I think, Slots? I think this is a little rich spoiled bitch that enjoys playing head games."

I tossed a sawbuck on the table and got up.

"Thanks, Stash. I still owe you a real lunch."

"Glad I could help," he said. "Straighten anything out for you?"

"Just the opposite, my friend. Just the opposite."

I walked back to the office and listened to the message on the machine.

It was Ackerman. "Your boy took the next day's flight out of Mexico and landed at Kennedy at six P.M., December seventh. Happy to help you, Slots old boy. I expect you to do the same for me in the future. I hope you get enough out of this to make a payment on that fancy Porsche of yours," he cackled.

*   *   *

The building housing Marsh Associates was a three-story brownstone in the high-rent seventies off Park Avenue. A brass nameplate had the name MARSH etched onto it and it was affixed to the door near the buzzer. A TV security camera's unblinking eye looked me over and the lock on the door clicked open.

When I called, the secretary had told me that Mr. Marsh would be in conference all afternoon. I told her to tell him that it had to do with Augie Casillo and he'd want to know what I found out. She had put me on hold, then, sounding somewhat surprised, she said Mr. Marsh would see me at two.

I approached the reception desk and an efficient-looking lady in her fifties wearing bifocals looked up from her word processor.

"You are Mr. Resnick," she stated.

"Yes."

"Won't you have a seat? Mr. Marsh will be right with you." She pressed a button on her desk and said, "Your two-o'clock appointment is here."

I gave Marsh credit for the interior decorating. Judging by the reception area, it looked like a place where big money could be made. Everything was richly understated: heavy furniture, dark wood paneling, functional and very expensive crystal chandeliers. Not an iota of plastic or glitz. It reminded me of the old banks that declared their rock-solid stability through concrete and marble. You got the feeling that if someone dared to speak above a whisper, there would be people coming around to shush you.

I thought Marsh would be coming out of one of the suites of offices down the hall beyond the receptionist. All of the doors were closed, and although I could see nameplates on the doors, I was too far away to read them.

Instead, Marsh came halfway down a wine-color-carpeted staircase.

1 3 3

"Mr. Resnick, please follow me. Thank you, Mary," he said to the receptionist, who smiled at him.

Marsh was wearing a blue serge suit, very expensive and well tailored, over a white silk shirt and a Windsor-knotted, muted-gold silk tie.

His office was a continuation of the downstairs motif except that behind his mahogany desk was a substantial library of impressive hardcover books, most of them dealing with finance.

He didn't sit behind his desk. Instead, he sat down on one of two chairs that looked as if they should have been in Buckingham Palace. I took the one opposite his. There was a large globe of the world in one corner of the room, near a worktable containing a FAX machine, an IBM computer, and some other hardware I wasn't familiar with.

Marsh reached into his pocket and brought out a gold cigarette case, flipped it open and held it out toward me. "Care for a smoke? They're imported from Europe and they're quite good if you like strong cigarettes," he said.

"I gave it up," I told him. "There's a rumor around that they're bad for your health."

"Really? One shouldn't pay attention to rumors. I happen to know that there are many more people who smoke and never get sick than there are people who do. I like the odds. Now, you told Mary you had some news on Casillo, I believe."

He set fire to his cigarette with a lighter he reached for from his desk. He also took an ashtray and placed it on his lap.

"I just got back from Mexico, where I traced Augie to the clinic."

"Yes, I know."

I stared at Marsh for a moment.

"Do you mind telling me how you know? You didn't have someone following me, by any chance? A fellow with white hair?" I kept my voice level, in keeping with the decor.

"Of course I wouldn't have you followed. Why on earth would I want to do that? My wife told me that she spoke to you at the Hard Rock Café."

"I find that hard to believe. She went to great lengths so you wouldn't find it out."

"I'm not surprised." He sighed. "At any rate, that's what happened. You can call her and ask her yourself."

Marsh looked squarely at me. Nothing suggested he was lying.

"Did she tell you what we talked about?"

"Yes. She told you that she thought I had killed Augie. She called me cold and calculating. Why do you look so surprised, Mr. Resnick? Surely you've figured out my wife by now."

"I've got some ideas, but I'd much rather hear yours."

Jeremy dragged on his smoke and delicately flicked the ashes in the ashtray with one finger.

"Cynthia is mentally disturbed, Mr. Resnick. She's not responsible for what she does or says. I'm sure you've already had her checked out through your police contacts and found she has an extensive arrest record. You can call her what you like—paranoid, schizophrenic, manic-depressive, drug addict, alcoholic, there's a whole dictionary of psychological terms to describe Cynthia's condition, and believe me, she's had the best psychiatrists in the world trying to treat her.

"Did I also mention nymphomaniac? She delights in having one-night stands and then torturing me with the graphic details. She can be very, very cruel."

I couldn't tell if Marsh was taking a shot at me. I ignored the implications.

"Why stay with her then?"

"For a childishly simple reason—I love her. She's the only woman I've ever loved or ever could love. She knows this and she punishes me. She believes she's horrible and worthless and will go to any extreme, do the most hurtful things, so I will leave her or throw her out. She must constantly test my love so she can be sure that I still love her. Can you understand this at all, Mr. Resnick?"

"I'm trying. It must be pretty tough to hold your temper sometimes. Don't you have a boiling point?"

"No, quite frankly, I don't. I think anger is a poor way to deal with problems. Anger obscures logical solutions. Of course, what you're really asking me, Resnick, is how did I feel about Cynthia's affair with Casillo, and would I be angry enough to kill him?"

"The thought did cross my mind."

"The answer is no, Mr. Resnick. The only person Cynthia truly loves is me. Whatever she does with someone else is only part of her psychosis. She does crazy things to test herself and me. She doesn't seem to feel alive unless she's experiencing some element of danger. Then she'll run back to me, confessing, weeping, and begging my forgiveness."

He sighed, started to say something, and then thought better of it.

"Augie Casillo called your house the day his wife died. Did you take the call?"

"No."

"Then Cynthia did. Supposing Augie said he felt guilty and didn't want to see her anymore . . ."

"Cynthia wouldn't like anyone walking out on her. She's the one who does the walking."

"Is she capable of killing someone?"

Jeremy thought about his answer. "I'm not sure," he finally said.

Trying to hire me to get to the bottom of a case in which she was the guilty party would certainly qualify as living dangerously, walking the tightrope without a net.

"She said she showed you a letter from Augie that said his wife had died, and you told her that she would never see him again. The implication was that you had him killed."

"Mr. Resnick, if I were a jealous man and resorted to murder, I might have to murder a good deal of the male population of Manchester, Connecticut, even including yourself, perhaps. What I meant was that it was obvious to me that Augie Casillo wouldn't return because of his debt. It's my business to loan venture capital. You get to know something about people when you make those decisions, and make no mistake about it, you loan to the people behind the corporation and not to the corporation. My gut feeling was that Augie Casillo would never repay the loan, and hence never return."

"But he did return. He made it to Kennedy Airport on December seventh."

Marsh's eyebrows went up. "Interesting."

"Did you ever have Cynthia followed?"

"Of course. I hired a detective agency to keep track of her and try to keep her out of trouble. It was the Burnside Agency, on Madison."

"Was one of the people keeping tabs on her a middle-aged man with stark-white hair?"

"I don't know. I've never met any of the Burnside people."

"How's that?"

"I wasn't really interested in what she did, Mr. Resnick. I was only concerned that she didn't hurt herself, or others. I asked the Burnside people to be like body-guards or chaperons, if you will. I've never asked them for a report, so I never met any of their people."

"And Cynthia knew about this?"

"Oh yes. It was a great game for her to lose her body-guards. I hired them about a year ago and they've been a great source of comfort to me. I was always afraid that one night she'd overdose or throw herself off a bridge."

F. Scott Fitzgerald's line about the rich being very different from you and me buzzed around my brain.

"Mr. Resnick, do you have any hard evidence that something happened to Casillo?"

"No, it's just strange that a man comes back to the States and doesn't do anything with his house."

"Yes, but that in itself constitutes nothing. My offer about the money he owes me still stands. It's worth a third of whatever you collect."

"I'm not interested in that line of work," I said.

Take that, Ackerman!

The first chance I got, I called Cynthia Marsh. She confirmed everything Jeremy had told me.

"I do crazy things sometimes, I say crazy things. I'm sorry."

I persisted, but that was just about the best explanation I was going to get.

"If you come out here, we can talk more," she purred.

"That's okay. Jeremy said that you really love him. Is that true?"

"He's my anchor. He's the only person in the whole world who really gives a damn about me."

"Did Augie Casillo call you the day Theresa died?"

"No."

"You're sure?"

"Of course I'm sure. That son of a bitch used me. He used me to get money from Jeremy and then he skipped out on us both."

"How come you didn't lend him the money?"

"I don't have any money. Jeremy takes care of all my money. That was what the judge ruled."

Jeremy had taken control of her assets after a competence hearing. Probably after her stay at Bellevue.

"I have to hang up now, Slots. I'm sorry if I did anything wrong."

"One more question. That man with the white hair, how long had he been following you?"

"Just that day. He was a new one," she said.

* * *

I spoke to Larry Burnside of the Burnside Agency.

"Hello, Slots, how are you doin'?" Larry said.

"Jeremy Marsh says he hired you guys. Is that on the level?"

"Best client I ever had. Doesn't want a report, doesn't bust chops, pays his bill on the first of the month."

"What does he get for his money?"

"He doesn't want the doll to get hurt, or get in trouble. Shit! Let me tell you, though, she's a handful. Hey, but you ought to know that. I heard you shared a few moments with her at the Hard Rock."

"You had a tail on her?"

"Of course. I'm not going to cheat the old man out of his dough. He doesn't want to see the reports, but I still got to check up on my guys."

"Is one of your guys middle-aged with white hair?"

"Are you crazy? I got two guys, Geronimo Lopez and Al Maisel. They blend into the woodwork. You can bang right into them and you wouldn't know they were there. What the hell would I hire a guy with white hair for? He'd stick out like a Caucasian on a pro-basketball team."

"How long you been on the job with the Marshes?"

"'bout a year. What's the score?"

"Nothing really, Larry, just some background stuff. Thanks."

"Anytime, Slots."

Marsh never got Augie's call . . . Cynthia never got Augie's call . . . and yet the switchboard at Nueva Día registered that he spoke for eight minutes to the Marsh house in Connecticut.

There was also the call to Newark. A five-minute call to Jeff Davis.

12

. . . .

I drove back to Davis' apartment building and renewed my acquaintance with the doorman. A fin
bought me the news that Davis wasn't at home.

"Smokey's?"

"I don't know. He left early this morning. Could be,
though."

"You ever see him come in with a white guy with
white hair?"

"Nope. I don't think he's got any white friends. He's
a prejudiced spade, that one is."

I peeled off another five and gave him my card. "Put
a message on my Answerphone when he comes back
in."

"You got it. Just make sure you leave me out of everything. I don't want any trouble from that guy."

I gave Smokey's the once-over and there was no sign
of the big guy or his two thug pals. I was glad about
that. I didn't need a rematch.

On a hunch, I asked the bartender if Whitey was in
yet. What other nickname would a guy with white hair
have?

The bartender looked puzzled. "Only Whitey I see here is you, mister," he said to guffaws from a couple of barflies.

I was getting to be a big hit at Smokey's. I laughed along with the bartender to show I could take a joke.

I handed him my card. "If you see Jeff Davis, it's important that he get in touch with me."

"Sure thing," he said, putting the card on the bulletin board behind him.

I drove crosstown to the Manhattan North Precinct and brought up a cup of black coffee and a couple of Dunkin' Donuts for Stash. He was due back in a half hour, so I wound up giving away his coffee to his partner, J. J. Mitchell.

J. J. had stopped a bullet in the Ned Pinto case and it was damn good to see him at one hundred percent.

"How's Denise?" I asked him.

"Man, Slots! That woman can spend money! I bring home my paycheck and it's out of my hands and gone before I get a chance to let the damn ink dry."

"That's what happens when you get another kid. Let's see some pictures."

"I just happen to have a couple," J. J. said, opening up his desk drawer and piling pack after pack of photographs into my hand.

"So this is the famous Chelsea Mitchell." I looked at a very attractive two-year-old black child who seemed to enjoy mugging for the camera. "The kid's definitely a Miss America candidate."

"Bullshit, Slots! That kid is Miss World!"

"She would be, but there's this little bit of your looks there that might hurt her chances."

Stash's half hour dragged on to forty-five minutes.

J. J. offered to help, if he could. "What do you need, Slots?"

"I don't know, J. J. I wouldn't want to put you in a position where you might get hurt. Vargas and Ackerman would have a fit if they knew that you guys were giving me a hand."

"Hey, man, later for them. I don't forget who gave me my first break. Wasn't for you, man, I'd still be in Coney Island rousting drunks under the boardwalk."

"There's a stiff in Mexico City who tried to ice me. I don't have any idea who he is. I dummied up for the local yokels, but now I'd like to get a line on the creep. He's a middle-aged Caucasian, with snow-white hair. The guy in Mex who's handling the squeal is named Maldonato, he's a lieutenant. His partner is Luis Reyes. I need to get a set of the stiff's prints and have them run through the computers."

"Slots, I got me a contact in Mexico. It should be a cakewalk, but man, you know how they operate. It's always mañana, unless there's an incentive."

"How much incentive do you think this will take?"

"Give me a hundred and I'll see if it's enough. If they want more, I'll lay it out."

I handed J. J. a C-note. "I appreciate this, J. J."

"Hey, it's nothin', man. I'd be pissed if you didn't ask me."

I thanked J. J. and walked down the precinct stairs. Looking at little Chelsea had made me think about Arthur. Father Quinn had hired me as a gesture for Arthur to try to clear Davis' name in a baseball incident. Now there were two men dead in Mexico and possibly a third one—Augie Casillo. Instead of clearing Arthur's dad's name, I might be putting him away for life.

There was a pay phone near the door. I looked up Theda's number and told her to bring Arthur and Father Quinn to my office in the morning. She wanted to know what was up, but I put her off with some vague reference to important developments.

I then tried my office and used the Touchtone code to activate the phone machine. The only message was the one I had been waiting for. The doorman's nervous voice told me that my friend was back.

Outside, snow was falling rather rapidly, giving the streets that confectioners-sugar look. I held my topcoat closed and knifed my way through the wind to my car. I could think of a whole bunch of things I'd rather be doing than driving in a snowstorm to interview Jeff Davis.

I took a shot that the Brown Coats wouldn't be working in the snow and parked my car at a hydrant across the street from Davis' place.

A different doorman was on duty and this ramrod-straight Irishman didn't look like the type to play fun and games. He stopped me and asked whom I was going to see. I told him Davis and he pressed the buzzer on 12-C.

"Yeah?"

"What's your name?" the doorman asked.

"Mitts," I said, remembering Davis' buddy at Smokey's.

"A Mr. Mitts."

"Oh, Mitts, huh? Okay, send him up."

I rode the elevator to twelve, got off and stepped onto a threadbare gold carpet, and found the C-line. I rang the bell.

"It's open," Davis hollered.

I stepped into what used to be called a batchelor pad in the days when *Playboy* was hot stuff.

I had to let my eyes get adjusted to the pink-and-red light bulbs that made everything in the room fuzzy. There was a leopard-skin rug, a circular sofa, projection TV (the old kind with the projection box in front of the screen), a stereo now playing a female blues singer, and the strong smell of incense.

Davis was in the bathroom, his back to me. He was wearing a pair of boxer shorts while he shaved with a straight razor.

"Get me a brew from the fridge, Mitts," he said, scraping the long razor across his cheek.

I opened the bedroom door before I found the kitchen. I would have bet I'd see a water bed and a mirrored ceiling. I would have collected.

The kitchen had a table and a couple of plain wooden chairs. Not much action in that room, I supposed. The refrigerator was empty except for a six-pack of Old Milwaukee.

I pulled one off the plastic top and walked it over to Davis. "Here you go," I said.

He whirled around, furious, holding the razor menacingly in his hand. "Goddamn you, Resnick! I could cut you in two for this bullshit trick. I'd just say you were trying to rob me."

I pulled out my .38 and jammed it in his belly. "Do it, bastard! Let's see if you could slice my throat before I pull the trigger."

The ominous razor was in his right hand, the long straight edge poised ten inches from my jugular. We stared at each other like prizefighters trying to psyche out their opponents before the opening bell. We froze in that tableau for at least twenty seconds, then Davis slowly turned back to the mirror, lathered up the still-stubbled side of his face, and started shaving again.

I put the gun back in the shoulder holster.

"Whatever you have to say, say it and get out!"

"What happened to Augie Casillo? He's been missing for the last three years."

"I told you I'm not interested in proving that I didn't load up the ball. I don't give a shit about Augie Casillo."

"You better give a shit, because we're not talking about cheating in a baseball game, we're talking about murder!"

Davis looked at me through the mirror. "What are you talking about?"

"Somebody followed me to Mexico and came at me with a gun when I started asking questions about Casillo. Somebody doesn't like the idea that I'd like to find Augie. It bothers them so much that they tried to kill me. I'd say that's a good indication that Augie is long gone."

"What does that have to do with me?"

"Augie called you from Mexico after his wife died. What did he tell you?"

"You're nuts! I never spoke to the man."

"I've got proof that you did. You also popped off that you were going to kill him. You told that to a group of sportswriters and to a television audience."

"So I got a bad temper. I was sore."

"What were you sore about if you were guilty?"

"What do you mean? I was angry I got caught."

"Funny how you stopped being angry right around the time Casillo disappeared."

"Resnick, I'm going to tell you one more time to stay out of my life. You don't have a damn thing on me. If you had any proof of anything, you'd have given it to the cops. You're wasting my time—and yours," he said between clenched teeth. "NOW GET OUT OF MY APARTMENT!"

I backed away and walked to the door. When I turned the knob I placed the blues singer on the record. It was the great black artist Alberta Hunter. She had sung the lead in *Showboat* with Paul Robeson, had been the toast of Europe in the 1930s, and then retired from show business, only to be rediscovered when she was in her late eighties. I had been a fan of hers since I saw her perform at The Cookery in the Village.

It made me wonder how a guy with the taste in music for Alberta Hunter could put pink and red lights in his apartment for atmosphere.

13

I had trouble falling asleep, and once I did, I had trouble staying asleep. I wasn't looking forward to my meeting with my "clients."

Harry Quinn showed up first, and then Theda and Arthur on his heels. I sat them down around the desk and told them what had happened in Mexico. Arthur's eyes opened wide as I related my brush with death. Harry grew thoughtful and Theda looked bewildered.

"What does all this mean?" she wanted to know.

"It means a heck of a lot more than we bargained for," Harry told her dejectedly.

"I'd say it's a pretty good indication that the reason no one has heard from Augie Casillo for the last few years is that he's dead. I was getting close to something and the killer or killers were getting nervous."

"Who was the man with the white hair?" Arthur asked.

"I'm hoping to find that out soon. Maybe today, if a friend of mine can come through."

"This makes it look bad for Jeff." Harry sighed.

"Why?" Arthur wanted to know. "My dad didn't do it!"

"Hold on, Arthur. No one is accusing your dad, and we don't even know if Augie really has been killed."

"But that's what you're thinking, right?" he said belligerently.

"I think Slots wants us to know all the facts," Quinn told him. "Your father did make threats against Casillo, that's a matter of record."

"He also was very adamant that he was innocent and wanted to prove to the world that he didn't doctor baseballs, and then suddenly he seemed to want to forget about it. That happened right around the time Casillo disappeared," I added.

"That's no proof!" Arthur yelled.

"We're not saying it is, son," Quinn tried to calm him.

"What about you, Slots? Do you think my father killed that man?"

"We're only talking about possibilities, Arthur. It's a possibility."

"You're a liar!"

"Arthur!" Theda reached for his shoulder, but he brushed her hand away.

"You're all liars. You all think it was my dad. I hate all of you. I HATE YOU!"

He got up from the chair and ran out of the office. I was the first one out of my chair to give chase but he had a big head start and the kid could motor. I gave up after a few steps.

Theda was crying. Harry had his arm around her and was trying to console her.

He patted her gently. "Everything's going to be fine. It's going to come out all right," he told her reassuringly.

"I'm sorry," I said.

Theda looked up after a moment and tried to smile. "It's not your fault, Mr. Res——, Slots. You're just doing the job Father Quinn hired you to do. I don't give a damn for Jefferson Davis, but I'm very worried about my boy. He's so hard to understand, I pray to God he . . ."

She tried fighting back the tears but the waterworks won out. The best I could do was to hand her a couple of tissues from the box I kept on my desk. No one had to mention it, but we were all thinking about Arthur's flirting with suicide.

The kid hadn't given me a chance to talk about the two others who had motives to kill Augie Casillo. I broke the silence and told them about Jeremy and Cynthia Marsh.

"So Jeremy could have done it," Quinn said.

"We don't know that anyone has done anything yet," I interrupted.

"I know that, Slots. I'm just supposin' now. This Jeremy character could have been jealous, and the missus—Cynthia—might have done it because Augie called to say it was over between them, or she could have killed him for kicks."

"If Augie is dead, Slots, who do you think did it?" Theda was dabbing at her eyes and looking to me for a definitive answer.

"To tell you the truth, there are flaws in all three of the motives. Jeremy is a very cool, detached character. I have a hard time thinking of him killing someone out of jealousy. His wife has had plenty of men in the past, and to my knowledge the streets of Manchester aren't littered with bodies. Cynthia, for all her complaining about her husband and her fooling around, is still very much tied to Jeremy. She tells him about her indiscretions, she looks to him for help, she doesn't seem the type to be attracted to another man so much that she would kill him for trying to break away."

"She does seem crazy, though," Theda interjected.

I nodded. "She's the wild card. There's no telling what she's capable of. But she's gone through all kinds

149

of trouble, and most of her hurting was done to herself and not to others."

"What about Jeff?" Quinn asked.

I shrugged. "It seems to me that Jeff is just the opposite of Jeremy. He would lash out right away. He's not the type to wait for months to get even. I'd think it would be hard for Jeff to sustain the anger it would take to murder someone."

"You're doing that setting-up-and-knocking-down thing again." Quinn sighed. "C'mon, Slots, if Augie is dead, who would you put your money on as the killer?"

"Not enough information for me, Father. I'd have to pass. There's something I'm missing."

"Would you take me home, Father?" Theda seemed to have aged ten years since walking into my office. "I want to see if Arthur went home," she said.

"Sure," Quinn agreed, retrieving their coats.

After they had gone I called up J. J. to find out if he had been able to dig up anything on my friend in Mexico.

"I was going to call you in a minute or two. They don't have a FAX machine in their office, so I can't give you the full report. My contact gave me the highlights, though. The guy's name is Joe Faine. Mean anything to you?"

"No, should it?"

"He's a contract man, works mainly on the West Coast. He's got a lot of arrests on suspicion, but no one could make them stick. Just before the trial, witnesses somehow disappeared. His going rate was five grand for a hit, but he's been known to kill for a hundred bucks just to keep his action going."

"He sounds like a hell of a nice guy," I said.

"A sweetheart. You were lucky, Slots. This guy usually connects."

"Thanks, J. J."

"No problem, and you got twenty bucks coming back to you from your C-note."

150

"Buy the baby some designer diapers," I told him.

I poured myself a bowl of raisin bran, which I had to eat with orange juice since the milk was sour. I was just starting to get used to the weird taste when the phone rang.

"Slots, it's Harry."

"Did the boy go home?"

"Nope, and Theda is beside herself with worry."

"I think he'll be all right. He just needs some time to think things out."

"I think it's a little more than that. He's developed a case of hero worship on you, Slots, and he thinks you've let him down."

I knew Harry was right.

"You know what they say about making an omelet, Slots."

"Yeah, but we're dealing with a kid and not an egg," I snapped.

I liked the kid more than I wanted to admit.

There was a long pause. Quinn was trying to make me feel better and I was biting his head off.

"Sorry, Harry. I guess all our nerves are on edge."

"No offense taken, Slots. The fact of it is that if you asked me who I'd bet on, it would be Davis."

"Stick with horses and football. Leave the detective business to—"

Damn! Why hadn't I thought of it sooner!

"Harry, you lovable bookie of a priest, you said you'd bet on Davis. Right?"

"So?"

"So how many people bet on Davis in that play-off game?" I asked him excitedly.

"I—I don't recall, exactly . . ."

"I guarantee you that it was the biggest line spread of the year. Davis was coming into the game on a roll. He had just pitched a couple of shutouts, I think he won six in a row. I believe the other team just put in a rookie. They were just about conceding the game. The line had to be two and a half or three to one."

"I have the records of that day at Capaldo's. Why don't you meet me there," Harry said. "Do you really think it might have a bearing—"

"You'll be the first to know!" I snapped.

There was more than wine stored away in Frankie Capaldo's wine cellar. Father Quinn had the records of four decades neatly stacked in his accountant's ledger books.

He walked slowly, looking at the bindings on the tomes until he came to the year we were looking for. He put the book under his arm and marched back up the stairs to his little office. The glasses came out of his pocket and shifted to the peak of his nose. His index finger darted to his mouth, and with a flourish he turned the pages.

"Aahh, *yes!*" he said.

I was looking over his shoulder and all I could see were jumbles of numbers and initials that made absolutely no sense to me.

"Uh-huh!" He was nodding.

"What? What do you see?"

"Sit down, Slots, and I'll explain."

I knew Quinn would make a production out of this. I hurriedly sat down.

"You're quite right, Slots my boy. That was the biggest spread of the year on a game."

"How big?"

"If you wanted Davis, you had to lay three to one."

"So if Davis loses, my hundred on the other pitcher—"

"That was Cal Winters," Quinn read.

"Yeah. If I bet on Winters, and I put up a hundred, you'd have to pay me three hundred, right?"

"Correct. I had one of my biggest days of all time. Everyone and his dog were betting on Davis. The whole world saw it as an opportunity to murder their bookie. When Davis got thrown out of the game and his team lost, bookies all over town were driving Cadillacs. You see, Slots, once the umpire says 'Play Ball,' you're stuck with your bet regardless of what happens on the field."

"I know, Harry. I didn't just come to the city on a pickup truck with a watermelon under my arm and some hay between my teeth. I already figured that a lot of bookies cleaned up. But I want to know about the guys that got wiped out."

"You mean bookies who got stuck with a lot of money on Winters?"

"I'm talking some serious money on Winters."

Quinn closed his eyes and I thought the old man was going to sleep. He wasn't—he was thinking.

"Yes!" he said excitedly.

"What, yes?"

"The Rabbi! The Rabbi got wiped out. I remember now."

"A rabbi? What the hell is going on? Has bookmaking become a new sideline for the clergy? What happened to bingo, for God's sakes?"

"No . . . no. He wasn't a real rabbi. He was Jewish, so they called him the Rabbi. Jackie 'the Rabbi' Glassman."

"He got hit hard because of this game?"

"Destroyed! He was the talk of the bookies for weeks. Now, anytime anyone loses big, they say they got the Rabbi's curse on them."

"Is he still around?"

"Around, yes. Bookmaking, no. He and his brother Sol own a men's clothing store on the East Side."

"Give me the address," I said, handing Quinn a piece of paper.

He wrote down the number. It was on Division Street, not far from Capaldo's.

"I better call him and tell you're coming. It's not

one of his favorite subjects to talk about," Quinn warned.

Glassman's Imported Men's Wear had a cluttered window featuring a lot of leather and suede and no prices. I had to wait by the door until someone buzzed open the lock.

A sour-looking man dressed in a blue suit was sitting in front of a rack of men's raincoats. He held a container of coffee in his hand.

"Good day," he said, rising. "What would you like to see? We got a great special on jackets. I think I got one that will fit you to a T."

"I'm Slots Resnick. I think Father Quinn called you."

"Who do you want to see?"

"Jackie Glassman."

"He's in Florida. I work here for him. You think a guy with his money is going to stay around here when he's got a condo in Florida worth maybe three or four hundred grand? He's going to stay here and bust his ass?"

"Is there a number where I can reach him?"

"I don't got no number. God forbid you should be a customer," he said disgustedly.

"I'm sure there's someplace he could be reached in an emergency?"

"Yeah, he calls in every other day."

"The next time he calls, please give him my number and ask him to call me. It's important."

The man looked at the card. "Okay, I'll do that."

I turned to go and made it to the door.

"Hey, Resnick, where are you going? Don't be a shmuck. I'm Jackie Glassman. I'm kiddin' you."

"You got a great sense of humor," I said sarcastically.

"I'm the life of the party. Look at this cup of coffee. Is this a container of coffee for a man? You got enough coffee here for three people. What the hell am I supposed to do with it? I drink this mud, I'll be pissing for a week. This is a goddamn container for a horse, not for a person!"

"Well . . ."

"So what do you want to know? You want to know how I single-handedly took my life and flushed it down the toilet bowl?"

"I'm interested in—"

"Yeah, I know. You're interested in the first play-off game, the famous Vaseline Game. The son of a bitches who give you so much coffee should only drop dead! Where was I? Oh, you want to know how a smart guy like me got wiped? Lookin' at me you can't believe it, right?"

"Hard to believe," I agreed.

"When my brother Sol heard the news . . . you know, that Davis was out of the game and we lost . . . he fell to the floor, the telephone still in his hand pressed up against his ear. I'll never forget that. Three guys had to pry that phone from his hand. He was lying there stiff as a board, totally freaked, making sounds like 'gah . . . gah . . . gah!' See, he was my partner in this thing. I didn't have the cash, so he put up his half of the store. This place was once a gold mine. You better believe it. We had every doctor in the city shop with us. Oy, but that was back in the good old days . . .

"So anyway, where was I? Oh, for maybe seven weeks before the game there's this broad, a redhead, long red hair, a knockout. Sol's tongue is hanging out from this doll. She says she likes to bet big money on sports. She's some kind of Duchess from some half-assed country like Luxembourg, or some shit. Now, we're not a big house. Me and Sol did a little gambling, had some bucks from the store, we put money out on the street and shylocked. . . . Everything was going good. Then the Duchess comes in and says she likes to bet big money on baseball. She wants to bet a hundred grand on the Dodgers on Monday-night baseball. Sol thinks he can handicap pitchers and he swears the Dodgers can't beat the Astros with Nolan Ryan."

"You wouldn't take a bet that size from a stranger?"

"Hey, what do I look like? I tell her that we got a store with a million bucks in inventory and we're going to be here tomorrow. How do we know you're going to pay up? She says that ain't a problem. She brings in a suitcase filled with money, maybe a half million bucks all in hundreds, and she counts out a hundred and ten thousand, the extra ten being the vigorish if she loses. We lay off half of the bet, and when the Dodgers don't win, we're up maybe fifty-five thousand. The next week she comes in, does the same thing. Bets a hundred grand and leaves it with us. Again she loses."

"How did she know you would pay off if she won?"

"First of all, Slotsy, we got a reputation to maintain. More important than that, she walks in with this monster man. The guy was so big he had to walk into the store sideways because his shoulders couldn't fit through head-on. Now she don't have to say a thing. She just buys this animal some clothes, and he's wild about her and snarling at everything else. Me and Sol don't have to be hit over the head to know that if we don't pay, Godzilla is going to be coming around.

"Well, like I said, she comes back week after week. We win some, we lose some. On the whole, we're about even. One week she puts down one hundred fifty thousand, another week she puts down two hundred, then back to a hundred. Like I say, we're going back and forth on the same money, except, with the vig, we're up maybe forty grand."

"Then came the big one?"

"Yeah. This week she comes in with a half-million. She says she thinks this Winters kid has a shot against Davis. She's going to crap-shoot with the full half-million on Winters. Sol can't wait to take the bet. He's jumping up and down. This is the score of a lifetime, he tells me. There's not an expert in the country who thinks Davis could lose. That big shwartzer is invincible, Sol says."

"So you made the bet?"

"No, I say what if we lose? Now we get the edge because anyone betting a half-mill is entitled to an extra point. She should be getting four to one instead of three, so we're ahead on that score. Trouble is, we can't cover a million-five if we lose. We can't lose, Sol says. How can we lose? We got about six hundred in cash, the store's worth another six, and we make a deal with one of the wise guys for another three hundred Gs if we lose. Of course, we can't lose. But we did!

"End of story. End of Sol. He's still in Bellevue going 'gah . . . gah,' and that's the story. She came back with Godzilla the next day and picked up most of the money. Godzilla punched a hole in the wall because we didn't have it all, and the next week we mortgaged our houses and the store and we paid her off. Never saw her again."

"Did you think the game was fixed?" I asked him.

He shook his head. "Not right then, but something happened. See, the story got around how the Rabbi got taken to the cleaners. One day this guy comes in and says his name is Tony Greco. He died last year, so you got to take my word on this. He took numbers and had a successful bookie operation in Long Island City. He asks about the Duchess and Godzilla. See, she would come to me and bet the Dodgers, and go to him and bet the Astros. Whoever played, she'd bet one team with me and the other with Greco. She had to beat one of us, and all it cost her was the vig that she paid when she lost.

"On the play-off game, she bet Winters against Davis with Greco, too. See, it cost her maybe seventy grand to set us both up. She walked away with three million. Greco to his dying day thought she lucked out, but I don't believe it. That Vaseline was a setup."

I pulled out the picture Cynthia had given me. I

157

looked at the four faces; Jeremy, Cynthia, Augie, and Theresa. Then I passed it over to Glassman. "Is that her?"

"Nah, she had long red hair. That's not her."

Near Glassman's cash register there was a red pencil. I colored Cynthia's hair and drew it longer.

"Take another look," I said.

This time Glassman reached into his pocket and put on his glasses. He stared a long time.

"Son of a bitch! That's the Duchess!"

14

I called Jeremy's New York number and impressed upon his secretary how important it was for me to talk with him. Reluctantly, she put me through.

Jeremy got on, sounding annoyed. I told him there were some new developments in the Casillo case and I asked him when he would be home. I explained that I had to talk to both him and his wife.

"Resnick, I'm beginning to find this whole affair tiresome," he told me in that snotty way of his.

"Fine. Then I'll go right down to your local sheriff and let him talk to you in public view at the Manchester Police Headquarters."

"Let's not get nasty, Mr. Resnick. You know very well that I can't have that kind of publicity." He sighed. "Could you be at my home at four?"

"That would be fine. What about Cynthia?"

"I'll see to it that she will be there. I hope this isn't a waste of our time. There are some very important negotiations about to take place and I'll need to conserve my time and energy for them."

I assured him that his time wouldn't be wasted.

I spent the rest of the afternoon looking for Arthur. The boy hadn't returned home and Theda was frantic with worry. I went around the block questioning some of his friends, who hadn't seen him but wanted to know what he had done. At the very least, when Arthur came home he'd be considered a hero because, as one kid put it, "the cops are lookin' for Arthur."

I even cruised around Davis' neighborhood, though, according to Theda, she didn't think Arthur knew Jeff's address.

Theda had told me that this wasn't the first time he had run away. He had done this once before and stayed away for two days. He was very street-smart and could take care of himself, but that didn't make things any easier on Theda.

Theda had been very gracious to me, under the circumstances, but I couldn't help feeling somewhat responsible for the kid's actions. I wondered if I could have handled the meeting better. I tried to get my mind off Arthur, and the best way to do that was to put the pieces together in the Casillo mystery.

The fact that Cynthia had made a killing on the playoff game changed things around. She and Casillo had been having an affair. She had been setting up Greco and Glassman for at least two months before they pulled the big scam. I discounted the guy Glassman called Godzilla. He was just a prop for Cynthia whom she'd probably rented from a local gym. He'd gone along for the ride and played his part.

I wondered if Cynthia and Casillo had planned this on their own or if Jeremy had been a partner. There had been at least a million dollars in "seed" money that Cynthia had used to set up the bookies. Where did it come from? One thing was certain. Casillo had definitely been in on the deal.

That meant that Davis had been telling the truth when he screamed about being framed. Then why did he change his story? Had Casillo and Cynthia paid him off? Was he really concerned about the Hall of Fame, or was it something else?

The white-haired man, Joe Faine, bothered me too. I had assumed he had been following Cynthia, but maybe I was wrong. I thought back to his actions at the Hard Rock. He had stared at Cynthia as she walked by, but so had every man with an ounce of blood and testosterone. I'd thought he was hiding his face in the menu, but what if he was really hungry and wanted a burger before he picked me out of the crowd? If Cynthia had hired him, he could have done the job right there in the café. She could have pretended he was a friend, called him over. In that cacophony of sound, who could have heard a shot from a gun pointed under the table?

That left two people, or possibly three, who might have hired Faine. Jeremy, Davis, or, if he was really not dead—Casillo.

Casillo was a long shot because he'd been out of sight for so long. If he was alive, would he want me dead so I wouldn't discover his role in the sting? There's a big jump from framing a pitcher to hiring a hit man.

That brought me to Jeremy. Jeremy had the brains and the money to figure out the scam and set up Greco and the Rabbi. He could have hired Faine to ice me so what happened to Augie wouldn't be discovered. Jeremy had the most to gain by having Augie killed. The umpire was having an affair with his wife, and with Augie out of the way, his share of the spoils—a third of three million—could find its tax-free way into his own pocket. He didn't need Smart Guy Resnick around to look under rocks and get him caught up in a murder investigation. In addition, Resnick was another guy who'd made it with his wife, and that didn't usually lend itself to a warm friendship.

I pulled into the circular driveway of Jeremy's home at exactly a quarter after four. Betty let me into the now familiar living room and again I left a trail in the thick carpet as I took a chair.

Jeremy and Cynthia made no effort to get up. He was in a very large cane chair, the kind last seen in the play *His Majesty O'Keefe*. He had a glass of brown liquid in his hand that I assumed was alcohol. Cynthia was on a lounge wearing a terry robe. Her hair was wet, as if she had just come out of the shower. She bent over to pick up a cigarette from Jeremy's gold case, which was on the black onyx coffee table, revealing that she was wearing nothing underneath the robe.

I forced myself to look back at Jeremy. He was checking his watch as if to show his annoyance that I was a quarter of an hour late. Jeremy Marsh was a very busy man.

"Mr. Resnick, I hope you will get to the point. My wife and I have a dinner engagement, and there are some business matters that I must attend to."

"I won't impose upon you any longer than I have to."

Cynthia took a long drag on her cigarette and purposely avoided my eyes.

"Someone tried to kill me when I was in Mexico looking into Augie's disappearance. It was the same man that you thought was hired by Jeremy to follow you, Cynthia."

That seemed to get her attention.

"Remember, Cynthia? That white-haired man? His name was Joe Faine."

"Resnick, I assure you that I hired no one but the Burnside Agency to ensure my wife's safety. If this fellow did something against you, take it up with Burnside."

"Maybe he wasn't following Cynthia. Maybe he was hired by someone to follow me."

"That very well could be, but what does that have to do with us?" Marsh asked. "You were a detective for many years. I've looked you up, Resnick. I'm sure in your line of work you make enemies."

162

"Why do you think he wanted to kill you?" Cynthia asked me, ignoring her husband.

"To cover up Casillo's murder."

The effect of my words on Cynthia was obvious. She ground out her cigarette angrily and stared at her husband. "If you did something to Augie!" She let the threat hang in the air.

"Shut up!" Marsh told her glaringly.

"My wife has a flair for the dramatic. It's part of her illness."

"Your wife also has a flair for acting. I understand she played the part of a Duchess."

That bombshell made Cynthia lean back on the lounge, covering her eyes with her hands, like someone with a splitting headache.

Jeremy never batted an eyelash. "What else do you think you know?" he wanted to know.

"Uh-uh. You show me yours, and then I'll show you mine."

"You know that my wife made some money betting. There's no law against placing a bet, Mr. Resnick. The law punishes the individual who takes the bet."

"We're not talking about betting here, Mr. Marsh. We're talking about fixing the outcome of a game . . . and murder."

Marsh stared at the smoke coming from his fancy European cigarette. "I believe you need a body before you can claim there's been a murder."

"You might know a little about that, too. I'm going to ask you again about the phone call Augie Casillo made to your house from Mexico the day before he arrived back. That was December the sixth, three years ago."

"I have no idea what you're talking about." Marsh shrugged.

"I never got a call from Augie," Cynthia said, shaking her head.

I believed her.

"I think you're wearing out your welcome, Mr. Resnick. You've made some allegations and some amusing inferences, but if I'm not mistaken, juries require facts. I will ask you to leave my home."

"I won't be going to a jury with this. There will be other people who have an interest."

"Really?" Marsh's eyebrows knit together.

"You are familiar with the term 'leverage,' aren't you? Well, I think I've got some leverage that's going to carry some weight."

"Such as?" Marsh said boredly.

"A guy like Jackie Glassman is connected, and so was Tony Greco. Bookmakers have their own pecking order, with the little guys laying off money with the bigger houses, and the bigger houses laying off to the major houses. You swindled three million bucks from them. They're not a jury. They don't need to prove guilt beyond a shadow of a doubt.

"Then there's the matter of Augie's disappearance. He's got no relatives, so no one has made a fuss over his disappearing from the face of the earth. Guess what? I'm going to give the newspapers and the local gendarmes everything I know. They'll be the ones to sweat you about Augie's phone call, and even if they get nowhere, Marsh and Associates will get some great publicity.

"There's lots of juicy angles. Augie's affair with Cynthia . . . the three-million-dollar sting . . . it's going to be a goddamned light show."

"Slots, you wouldn't?" Cynthia said.

I was "Slots" again, the lover, the friend.

"I've got this peculiar idiosyncrasy. I don't enjoy it when someone is trying to blow my head off with a sawed-off shotgun. I guess I'm funny that way."

For his part, the smug expression was wiped off Jeremy's puss.

"Last chance for you to talk to me, Jeremy. I walk out of this door with nothing, you're history."

164

"Damn it, Jeremy! I'm going to tell him," Cynthia shouted.

"Don't," Jeremy said weakly.

For the first time, he looked shaken.

"Jeremy had nothing to do with it. It was me and Augie. It was my scheme, it was my money. I talked Augie into it."

She walked to the bar and took out a bottle of Scotch and poured it shakily into a glass.

"Cynthia, you're not supposed to—"

"I need a drink, Jeremy!" she snarled. She drank it down quickly.

"We were talking one night about fixing sports. I don't know, something came on TV about some horse-racing scandal . . . anyway, Augie said you couldn't fix a baseball game because you'd have to include too many people. He said the only shot you had was to fix the plate umpire because he calls the balls and strikes and could walk a guy on any close pitch, but even then it wouldn't make much of a difference.

"I didn't give it much thought until one day on TV I saw this guy Davis pitching. There was a close play at first and this Davis went crazy. He acted like a wild man and he got thrown out of the game. I asked Augie if Davis was always that nuts, and he laughed. He told me the man was a head case, ready to fight with anyone, and not just on the field. Augie and the other umpires sometimes travel with a team when they're on the road. They eat at the same places, and drink at the same places, and even stay at the same hotels. Augie said that Davis was disliked by his own teammates because he was such a hothead.

"Then it came to me how you could beat the odds. The umpire can throw a guy out of a game. If the player was a powerhouse like Davis, that would give you some edge. It was Augie who came up with the Vaseline idea. He could put some in his pocket and then transfer it to the pitcher's glove. No one would spot it and everybody was thinking Davis was doing it anyway. Augie knew he'd put up such a squawk that he could kick him out of the game and we could clean up."

"Why do it? You don't need the money," I told her.

"For kicks, Mr. Resnick." That was Jeremy. "Just for kicks. That's what my lovely wife has dedicated her life to. She's rich, and spoiled."

"And bored living with you, Jeremy darling," she snapped.

"Now tell me what the phone call was all about?" I wanted to know.

"I never got a call. I mean it, Slots. Augie went to Mexico with Theresa. I think that's why he went along with the fix, so he'd be able to take care of Theresa. It came to a lot of money, and he was just about broke."

"I thought Jeremy gave him fifty thousand."

"I did. I took the money they won in the bet and . . . Look, Resnick, you have to give me your word that you won't discuss this or tell the authorities."

"As long as you're straight with me, I'll do the best I can to keep you out of it," I assured him.

"All right. I advanced Augie the money because I was making sure the three million was laundered. There's a corporation in the Grand Cayman Islands that I work closely with. It wouldn't do to have the IRS start wondering how Augie became such a wealthy man. Through this corporation the money would be turned into corporate bonds and—"

"Hold it, Jeremy! I know you're a financial whiz. I want to hear about the eight minutes Augie spent on the phone with one of you."

"I know nothing about that," he said.

I got up. "You're lying, Jeremy. Thanks for your time."

I made it to the door before he called me back.

"Resnick—hold it! You win. I'll tell you everything. But remember, you promised . . ."

166

"Let's hear it," I said.

"I'm going to tell you everything that happened. I hope you understand, darling." He looked at Cynthia, who seemed completely in the dark.

"I got Augie's call a day before he was to come back to the States. There was no great mystery involved. He told me that Theresa had just died and he was flying back to New York the next day. I sympathized with him on his loss. He asked me to do him a favor. He said he was going to sell the house. Living there would be just too painful. He knew we were having near zero weather, and he asked me if I would put the boiler on for him, so the next day when he arrived, the house would be warm enough for him to go through the papers he needed and collect some personal effects before he moved out of there for good. He didn't want to stay long, and he didn't want to freeze. It was something we used to do for each other. He had my keys, and I had his. I went over and put on the boiler as he requested."

"Why didn't you ever tell me about this?" Cynthia asked him.

"Because the rest of the story would be too painful for you."

"What is that supposed to mean?" Cynthia demanded.

"The next evening, Mr. Resnick, I returned from work. I decided to go to Augie's home and wait for him. He would soon have his money, and I wanted him to stay away from my wife. I was prepared to offer him an additional million if he would just disappear from Cynthia's life. She'd had many affairs, but this one lasted the longest, and quite frankly, I was jealous. I say jealous, Mr. Resnick, but not in the sense that someone else might use that word.

"Cynthia is really incapable of loving anyone, including herself. I am the only man who could put up with her, and care for her. I know her better than she knows herself. She'll never really leave me. She can only give her body, and those few moments of coupling with another man mean absolutely nothing to me. I want you to know this because a crime of passion would be preposterous for a man of my nature."

I looked at Cynthia. She was biting her lip and staring into the bottom of her glass of Scotch. I wondered what was going through her mind.

"You were going to visit Augie," I prodded.

"Yes. I walked down the road and when I approached the house, I heard loud shouting. There were two men arguing. I wasn't going to walk in on an argument, so I decided to wait until Augie was alone."

"What was the argument about?"

"I couldn't tell. You could just hear the loud angry voices. What they were saying was unintelligible. Then I heard a shot."

"Oh my God!" Cynthia breathed.

"The voices stopped, and there was complete silence. I was just off the road, so I could see the doorway. I didn't know what to do. I just waited. It was starting to get dark but there was a full moon and I could still make out the doorway and the front of the house. All of a sudden, a very big man walked out, carrying something over his shoulder. I couldn't make out what it was at first, then I realized it was Augie's body."

"Oh, God, no!" Cynthia cradled her head and began to cry softly.

If she was putting it on, she deserved an Oscar.

"Did you call the police?" I asked him.

"No . . . I didn't want to get involved. I . . . there was nothing I could do for Casillo. I couldn't afford the publicity. Then there was Cynthia's involvement. I just went home."

"That's all you did? You just went home?" Cynthia said incredulously.

"What did you expect me to do? I'm not a hero. I saw the way Casillo was lying over the man's shoulders. He was dead. I knew it! I went back an hour later. It had snowed much of the day and it had started again. I followed the man's footprints to the lake."

"What lake?" I asked him.

"There's a lake about thirty yards behind Augie's property," Cynthia said.

"The footprints stopped at the edge of the water, and then they led back to the house. This time they weren't as deep."

"Meaning that you think this man threw Augie Casillo into the lake," I said.

"Yes." Jeremy nodded.

"You son of a bitch!" Cynthia wailed. "You never told me. You never told me any of this!"

"Why would I want to hurt you? You were having enough problems with drinking and drugs. I couldn't risk you having a complete breakdown."

"Jeremy, you should have told me! For three years I've been expecting that phone to ring and for Augie to get in touch with me."

"It was better for you if you thought he had left you for good."

"You bastard! It was better for you, you mean!"

I interrupted. "Can you give me a description of this big man who carried Augie to the lake?"

"It was getting dark, and I couldn't see too well."

"How unfortunate," I said dully.

"But I did get something that might be of interest."

There was a picture of an old-time Yankee clipper sailing the waves. Jeremy pushed it aside to reveal a wall safe. He fiddled with the combination lock and then opened the safe. He reached in and brought out a piece of paper. He handed it to me.

"That's the license-plate number of the man's car. I wrote it down, just in case. It's a New Jersey license. Now, remember your promise to keep us out of this," he said.

I folded the paper and walked toward the door. "Yeah, I remember," I growled.

Cynthia was crying softly on the lounge chair.

15

· · · · · · · · · · · · · · ·

The town of Manchester was three blocks long and had all the essential ingredients of small-town America. There was a pharmacy, a school (Manchester High School), a grocery store, a combination burger place and frozen-custard emporium, a church, a movie house imaginatively named the Manchester Theater, a one-pump Mobil station, a partridge in a pear tree, and—what I was looking for—the sheriff's office.

This was a one-story white concrete affair with glass doors bearing the official crest of Manchester, the Connecticut state flag, and Old Glory. I stepped into a modern office that had been broken up into four separate cubicles and a main room where a man with a headset was communicating, presumably with officers in the field.

A pleasant-looking civilian looked up at me from a desk that had the sign STATE YOUR BUSINESS BEFORE PROCEEDING FURTHER, handwritten in black crayon, pasted to its front. The farthest cubicle from the door had the name SHERIFF PAUL BRADFORD written on a wooden plaque.

"I'd like to see Sheriff Bradford," I told her.

"Do you have an appointment?"

"No." I tossed my business card down in front of her. She picked it up, gave a quick glance and looked up. "Would you like to tell me what this is in reference to?"

"I think I have to discuss that with the sheriff."

I flashed my patented sorry-but-you-understand look and she walked my card back to Bradford's office and knocked softly on the door. She went in and when she came out a moment or so later, waved for me to come in.

The office was small and cluttered. Bradford was holding my card and talking on the phone. The receptionist closed the door behind her, and I took a hard wooden chair facing the sheriff.

He was about fifty-five, with steel-gray hair cut in a military crew cut, tanned craggy features, and a no-nonsense look behind cool blue eyes.

He placed the phone on the cradle and devoted his full attention to the card. "You're a private investigator, Mr. Resnick?"

"Business cards don't lie," I told him. "I think you've got a murder on your hands."

"Is that right?" the sheriff said.

His face broadened into a smile. "Now I know who you are! This Mickey threw me off. You're Slots Resnick, from New York. I thought you looked familiar."

"Do we know each other?"

"As a matter of fact, I saw you give a talk on Interrogation Procedure at the National Police Convention in Dallas about four or five years ago. I was pretty impressed. You were the top gun in New York. What happened?"

"Politics."

"Backed the wrong team?"

"Never learned how to play the game," I said.

"Well, you can never be a small-town sheriff then. I

been here almost fifteen years. I've run unopposed the last three elections. I came here from Chicago for a visit and never went back. That was back in the sixties. Married a local girl and had three kids. Who's been murdered?" he asked, switching gears.

"I've got a pretty good indication it's Augie Casillo."

"I thought he was in Mexico with his ailing wife."

"He was. Theresa died and Augie flew back to Manchester three years ago. I've got reason to believe he's in the lake on the property behind his house."

"You want to tell me how you've come by this information?"

"I guess I'll have to eventually, but I'd rather keep it to myself just now. There's always the chance that it won't pan out."

Bradford made a face. "I hate to pull them out of the water."

I knew what he meant. Every cop had a horror story about corpses taken out of water. Rookies had been known to faint and give up eating for days.

"You know who did it?" he wanted to know.

"I've got an idea, but nothing solid. I'd like to keep that to myself, too."

"Client?"

"No."

"Then you don't have that privilege, do you?"

"No."

I wondered what he would do. If he wanted to be a bastard, he could keep me on ice, search the lake and then practice some of my own interrogation techniques on me. I knew he was thinking the same thing.

"Y'know, Slots, I'm not above getting help. If what you're saying is true, this little town is going to be in the headlines. Usually, the biggest problem we have is a drunk-and-disorderly charge. I've got a lockup downstairs with three cells and they stay empty most of the week except for Saturday night, when Ollie Selig has five or six too many. I guess I'm getting around to the fact that if someone *did* do Augie in, what you know can make the difference in whether or not I get elected for another couple of terms."

"I know what you're saying. I'm not looking to make a reputation. You've got the inside just as soon as I know if there is a body in the lake."

Bradford picked up the phone and made a couple of calls. He lined up a couple of scuba divers and a local garage with a winch. When he was finished he asked me if I was going to hang around. I told him I had a few things to do, but I'd keep in touch.

"Say, Slots, I think it would be a good idea on both of our parts if we keep publicity down."

"That suits me," I told him. "You might want to get Augie's dental records."

"That's no problem. We've only got Doc Meyers. Everybody in town uses him, and that included Augie and Theresa."

"I'd like to use your phone, Sheriff."

"Sure, go ahead."

"Mind if I use the one outside?"

"You're a careful one, aren't you? Just go out and tell Phyllis I said it was okay. You can send her back here."

"Thanks."

I called J. J. and had him run a Jersey plate check on the license Jeremy had given me. It didn't exactly come as a shock to find out that the dark blue Buick Electra was registered to Jefferson Davis of Newark.

It took me an hour to hit the Bronx, and another hour on Morningside Drive as a result of a water-main break on the street near the exit ramp.

I had intended to drop in on Davis and give him a chance to turn himself in before he was arrested. I owed it to Arthur to try to help Jefferson work out some kind of deal with the DA. I wondered if the DA would go for a reduced charge if Jeff agreed to full co-operation.

That was before I turned on the radio and heard the bulletin:

174

Manchester, Connecticut, police report the finding of a weighted body in the Manitoa Lake today. Acting on a tip, Sheriff Paul T. Bradford discovered the badly decomposed body early this afternoon. Police sources tell us they believe the dead man is former major league umpire Augie Casillo. Please stay tuned for the latest in this breaking story.

So much for Bradford's trying to keep it quiet!

My newfound buddy, Davis' doorman, put the icing on the cake when he told me that Jefferson "came running out of here like a bat out of hell."

I nosed the Porsche downtown and made it to my office, hungry, frustrated, and tired.

Paul Bradford was on the phone answering machine and he sounded genuinely sorry. He explained that one of his divers had a brother who worked for one of the local radio stations and it was he who broke the story, much to Bradford's disgust.

I clicked off the machine and called Harry Quinn at the rectory. He hadn't heard the news and when I told him about Augie being found and Davis being implicated, there was a deafening silence on the other end of the phone.

"Y'know, Slots, I'm sorry I got you involved in this thing," Harry said. "I'm very fond of the boy, and I thought we could help him."

"Has there been anything from him?"

"He called his mother this afternoon and told her not to worry. He wouldn't tell her where he was, but he said he was all right. It was a bit of comfort for Theda, but now . . ."

"Well, so far no one has made the link between Augie and Davis. Maybe we can catch a break and I can talk Davis into cooperating with the DA in return for a reduced plea."

"I never knew you to be a long-shot player, Slots," Harry said with a sigh.

I hung up from Harry figuring my mood couldn't get worse. I was wrong.

The networks had picked up on the Casillo story and it was the lead on two of the three flagship stations. Both of them flashed pictures of Jefferson Davis, *former pitching great who was thrown out of a play-off game for doctoring a baseball and who subsequently quit the game. Police are looking to question Davis.* Then they rolled the old taped footage of Jefferson after the play-offs where he threatened to *get* Augie.

It was the way the public liked their news. It was crystal-clear and wrapped up in a pretty bow. Casillo was found dead, Davis had threatened him; ergo, Davis killed him.

Now here's Steve with the sports. How about those Rangers, Steve?

I left the TV blaring and pulled open the small fridge. I poured Rice Krispies into a bowl and reached for the orange juice again. It was becoming addictive. I finished up, rinsed the bowl, and walked back into the other room just in time to hear that the station had a new development in the Augie Casillo case.

It appears the colorful umpire had been shot before being weighted down and dumped in Lake Manitoa. Police tonight confirm that a pistol was found in the lake along with the dead body.

They wanted us to stay tuned for further details, and there would be *film at eleven,* but the driving and aggravation had made me tired. I decided to catch a few zzz's and, later on, fully rested, plan my next move.

What started as annoying little taps soon graduated into bass-drum banging. I sat up and looked at my watch. It was twenty to twelve. The banging at the door started up again.

"Who is it?" I called out.

"It's me, Arthur!"

I opened the door and Arthur rushed in past me.

"Hi," he said, taking a seat on the couch where I had been sleeping moments before.

"Hi yourself. Do you know how worried your mother has been?"

"I called her." He shrugged. "I know how to take care of myself."

I was about to launch a tirade when the kid stopped me in my tracks.

"They say the gun was my father's," he said.

"What gun?"

"The gun they took from the lake. You know, where the umpire was killed?"

"How do you know that?"

"I heard it on the news." He told me.

If, in fact, the gun did belong to Davis, it was the final act in the play.

"I think I'd better get you home, pal," I told him.

"You can't, not yet."

"Why's that?"

"You've got to help me prove my father didn't do it. You're very smart, Slots. You can do it!"

"Arthur, I—"

"I'm your boss, Slots. I hired you!" Arthur said.

I took a deep breath. "I'm sorry, slugger, but maybe your dad is guilty."

He shook his head no vigorously. "I know he's not. He told me he didn't do it and I believe him."

"You're talking about him on TV again."

"Nope. I talked to him live . . . in person."

"Where?"

"First you have to promise you'll try and help him."

"Arthur, this isn't a game. There are a lot of policemen out looking to bring your father in for questioning. There are a lot of reasons why your dad is the prime suspect. If what you say you heard about the gun is true, then you're going to have to face the fact that he probably is guilty."

"He's not!" Arthur insisted with all the conviction a thirteen-year-old can muster. "I know it!"

There was no sense arguing with him.

"Are you hungry? Have you eaten anything over the last couple of days?"

"Yeah, I ate all right."

"I could offer you Rice Krispies with orange juice. It's the new taste sensation."

Arthur made a face.

"Okay, now why don't you tell me where you saw your dad and what happened."

"First promise."

"I'll promise to listen with an open mind and then I'll do what I can. How's that?"

"Good. I found out a long time ago where my father lived. Lots of times I would go to his building and just watch him. I wouldn't talk to him because I was afraid that he'd get angry and chase me away, so I just watched him."

"That's where you've been the last couple of days?"

Arthur nodded.

"Do you know where Jefferson is right now?"

"I was in a candy store across the street from my dad's house. I heard the man on the radio say that they found that umpire guy in the lake and he was dead. Then I saw my father leave his house and I followed him. He took the train and he got off on Fourteenth Street. I was riding in the next car and I got off, too. He didn't see me. Then he went to an apartment on the second floor near First Avenue. I put my ear to the door and I heard him listening to the news and that's when I heard that they found his gun."

"Arthur, are you sure you're not playing some kind of pretend game?"

"I swear, Slots, I'm telling you the truth," he said solemnly.

"Okay, I believe you. When did you talk to him?"

"After a while, I knocked on the door. He wouldn't answer. I knew he thought it might be the police, so I knocked again. I told him it was me, Arthur. I kept knocking until he opened the door and pushed me inside."

"He pushed you?"

"Well, he grabbed my arm and pulled me, and then shut the door real quick. He wanted to know what I was doing there. I told him that I had followed him and he got real angry. I told him that he didn't have to worry because I wouldn't tell anybody where he was.

"He gave me some money and told me to buy him some food, and a bottle of gin, and come back . . . which I did. Then we talked for a long time and he told me that he didn't do it, you know . . . kill that man."

"Go on," I said. I didn't doubt a thirteen-year-old could buy liquor. A ten-dollar bill had the ability to make a kid look twenty-one.

"He said that everyone would think he did, but it wasn't true. I told him about you. I said that you could help him. I said you were my friend and you wouldn't call the police on him."

"I can't see him believing that."

"Well, he didn't, at first. But I finally convinced him. He told me to bring you to him."

The whole story sounded implausible, but so implausible that it might be the truth. I could picture Davis feeling cornered, unable to leave a borrowed apartment, desperate for help. Then along comes his hero-worshiping kid, and Davis trusts him. Maybe he was so desperate that he was even willing to trust me.

"He told you to take me back to him?"

"Yes."

"Arthur, I don't want you to be upset if when we go back, he's not there," I warned.

"He'll be there," Arthur said. "My dad wouldn't lie!"

16

. . . .

We took the East River Drive and made it down
to Fourteenth Street in ten minutes. It was
after midnight and the roads were clear.

Arthur sat quietly, his hands in his lap, staring out
the window. Just before we left, I had secretly called
Theda and told her not to worry because Arthur was
with me.

"I heard about Jefferson on the TV," she told me. "If
Arthur finds out, it's going to break his heart."

"He knows, and he's okay. I'll bring him back as
soon as I can."

"Thanks, Slots. You've been a good friend."

We headed off the exit and I drove along Fourteenth
looking for the apartment building Arthur said he
would remember.

"Over there!" He pointed to a second-story window
in a four-floor tenement building next to a movie theater and a bodega.

The doorknob of the downstairs door had been
ripped out for its brass, leaving a hole through which

someone had put a small rope, making it easier to open the door. The hallway was dark and dingy. Someone may have swept it once since the Great Depression, but that was debatable. A loud-hissing radiator and the strong smell of urine completed the ambience.

"You're sure this is the place?"

"Yes, he's on the next floor. Come with me."

Arthur led the way up a creaky wooden staircase and knocked on a door with a "2" stenciled in paint. There was no response, so Arthur knocked again.

I was wondering if Davis had pulled a vanishing act on the kid when a voice in the apartment called out, "Who is it?"

"Me," Arthur responded.

There was the clanging metal of chains and locks being opened and then the door moved a crack. An eye took us in, then looked past us for anything lurking on the staircase. When he was convinced we were alone, Davis opened the door. We stepped in quickly and Jefferson closed it behind us.

He was wearing a blue sweat suit with sneakers and held a tire iron in his hand.

The apartment was a three-room railroad flat that looked as if it had been vacant a long time. In the center of the front room was a bridge table and four folding wooden bridge chairs. In the corner of the room was a dirty mattress, lumpy with uneven springs. Each of the three windows had drawn black shades and the only light was coming from a naked bulb above the table.

"Did he call the cops?" Davis asked Arthur.

The boy shook his head. "You can trust Slots," he said.

"One thing you better learn fast, boy, is you don't trust nobody," Davis said, staring at me.

"I'm here at your invitation, Jeff."

"You're here because the boy thinks you might be able to help me," he said, sitting at the table.

We joined him.

I knew he was using Arthur as a cop-out. He was desperate for my help, but too proud to ask. His face was drawn and his eyes were red and dilated. In addition to alcohol, there was the faint smell of marijuana.

"I didn't kill Casillo," Davis stated bluntly. "I'm being set up."

"Who's setting you up?"

Davis acted as if he didn't hear me. He rubbed his eyes with his hands and then stared at Arthur. "This fool kid's been followin' me and lookin' at me for years now. What you want, boy?" he asked angrily.

Arthur just shrugged. "Nothing."

"He wants a little recognition from his father. The kid idol-worships you, Jefferson. I don't know why, but he does. It's too bad you can't give something back. A kind word would go a long way."

He glared at me, and for one brief moment I thought he was going to use the tire iron to part my skull. Instead, he cradled his head and said softly, "You don't know shit."

"Who's setting you up?" I asked again.

"I don't know. I didn't kill Casillo. He was dead already," Davis mumbled.

The booze and the grass were making him drowsy. I shook him and snapped him awake.

"Listen, Davis, maybe as far as you're concerned I'm not much, but outside of me and Arthur, there's no big army of support. Before you go beddy-bye on us, you better give us something to go on or you'll be doing your sleeping in a four-by-four at Attica."

I let that sink in, and Davis seemed to make a visible effort to get his wits about him.

"What do you want to know?"

"Just tell me everything, exactly the way it happened. Don't leave anything out or try to bullshit me. I promised Arthur I'd listen with an open mind, and if I

1 8 3

felt you were leveling with me, I'd do what I could to help."

"Okay—okay."

"Tell me about the phone call."

Jeff nodded. "You're right, I did get a call from Casillo. I was sitting home watching television in the afternoon and I pick up the phone and it's Casillo. The first thing he says to me was that his wife died. He sounds funny, like he's been crying. I said that's too damn bad, but it should have been him.

"I can't believe the son of a bitch was calling me to tell me his old lady passed on. I cussed him out real good and all the time he don't say nothin'. After I'm finished, he says that he's got to talk to me. He says there's something he's got to tell me. I tole him, I'm listenin'. No, he says he got to see me in person. I says look, you mother, I don't want nothin' to do with you. I slammed down the phone."

"Did he say when he wanted to see you?"

"Yeah, he said he'd be home at seven the next night."

"But you did wind up going?"

"Hell, yeah! I got curious. I wanted to see what he wanted. I got there at seven and I found him. He was already dead."

"Tell me exactly what happened."

Davis shrugged. "Look, man, I don't know. I walked over to the door and it was half open. I knocked and then I walked in. Casillo was sitting at the kitchen table with his back to me. I said, 'I'm here, now what you want to say?' He don't move. I walk over and touch him and he falls on the floor. Then I see that he's been shot in the head.

"On the floor there's this gun. I figure he killed hisself. I'm lookin' around for a phone to call the cops, and shit, I look at the damn gun! I can't believe it, it's my gun! I get scared, see. Then I figure it out. His wife died, and he don't want to live no more, so he decides to check out and he wants to take me with him. He kills hisself with my gun and there's no suicide note or anything and it's going to look like I offed him."

"Why?"

"Shit, I don't know. You seen the tape of me on TV. I look like I could kill the bastard. Maybe that's how he got even. Maybe he even thinks I got his wife sick. Shit, I ain't no mind reader!"

"How did he get your gun?"

Davis shrugged. "I don't know."

"What are you giving me?" I said, annoyed.

"I'm tellin' you the truth, man! I got a permit for the gun and I take it with me when I'm on the road. I never knew it was gone until I seen it on Augie's floor."

"That doesn't make sense."

"I know that, bro! What do you think was going through my mind? Here's this guy dead after I go on national TV and threaten him, and he's shot with my gun!"

I remembered what Jeremy had told me about a loud argument.

"You never got a chance to say anything to him?"

"Hey, Slots, the last dead guy that got up and talked was Jesus. I don't know anybody else who could pull off that little trick."

"There's a witness who says he heard you arguing with Casillo."

"Bullshit!"

"Do you know anybody named Marsh . . . Jeremy or Cynthia?"

"Nope."

"This witness says he saw you pick up the body and carry it to the lake."

Davis reached into the pocket of the sweat suit and pulled out what was left of a bottle of gin. He took two large swallows and then wiped his mouth with the back of his hand.

"Yeah, 'cept I didn't know there was a lake there. I was just walking around looking for a place I could hide the body until I could figure things out. Then I found the lake. Shit, I figured I'd dump him in and that would be it. I stuffed his clothes with rocks and stuff and I waded out as far as I could—"

"What about the gun?"

"I tossed it away in the water."

"Why would you want to throw the gun in the lake?"

"Shit, man, I'm tellin' you I thought it was a setup. I couldn't take the gun with me. What if the cops were told to stop my car? They'd find the damn gun!"

"You waded into the lake with your clothes on in the middle of winter?"

"Yeah, my fear kept me warm," he said angrily.

"The lake wasn't frozen?"

"No, man. There was snow coming down but the lake was not frozen."

"Then what did you do?"

"I got in my fuckin' car, put the heat on full blast, and shivered my ass all the way back to Newark."

"And that's it? You didn't send somebody by the name of Faine to kill me?"

"That's everything, man. I don't know a Faine."

Davis finished what was left in the bottle.

I thought it over. Would Augie have wanted to kill himself after his wife died? He hadn't been so attached to her that it prevented him from having an affair with Cynthia. Then Jeremy claimed that he'd heard arguing and a shot. He didn't say he actually saw Davis.

"Slots, you will help my dad, won't you?" Arthur asked me.

"It's a tough story to believe," I said.

Davis smirked. "Sure you got an open mind?"

I ignored his sarcasm. "You didn't see or hear anybody else?"

"There was nobody else around."

"A man named Jeremy Marsh is willing to testify that he heard you arguing, he heard a shot, and he saw you carry out the body and throw it into the lake."

"The man was dead, Slots! There was nobody around. What the hell would anybody be doing out near Casillo's house anyway? There was a damn snow-storm going on."

"He claims he put on Augie's boiler the day before and then went over to say hello when he heard the two of you."

"He didn't hear shit."

Davis was rock-solid in his story. It would be his word against Jeremy's. There was also the mysterious way Davis' gun had appeared in Casillo's home. And Davis' nationally broadcast threat. Even if Jefferson was telling the truth, I wouldn't want to be his defense attorney.

Yet Davis had had three years to polish up his story. If this was his best shot, he had a crummy imagina-tion—or he was telling the truth.

"What are you going to do, Slots?" Arthur looked at me with those big eyes.

"He's going to walk out of here and call the cops," Davis said disgustedly.

"He will not!" Arthur said indignantly. "Will you?"

"No. I'll check out your dad's story."

When Jefferson mentioned calling the cops, some-thing connected.

"I'm going to go back to Manchester. I want you to go home," I told Arthur.

He shook his head. "I'm staying with my dad!"

Davis stared at the kid. It was hard to know what was going on in his mind.

"What do you say?" I asked him.

"The kid can stay. I may need him to pick up food for me," Davis said coldly.

Arthur didn't seem to notice.

"Who else knows about this place?"

I didn't want Arthur caught in the middle of a shoot-out.

"An ex–lady friend who don't know I got the key,

and who won't be back for another week. If there's heat, it's going to come from you."

I didn't press my point with Arthur. I didn't have the time to take him home, and knowing him, he'd just run back to his father again. Theda thought he was okay, and if Davis was right, nobody would drop in on them for at least the time it would take me to go to Manchester and back.

There was one very big hole in Davis' already implausible story. If someone had gone to the trouble of stealing Jefferson's gun to make it look as if Jefferson had killed Augie, or even if Augie did kill himself and had tried to make it look as if it were Davis who did it, where had the cops been? It would stand to reason that someone, Augie or the murderer, would have called the cops hoping that they would catch Davis standing over the body. Who could know that three years later Slots Resnick would be snooping around?

I thought about the Marshes and Davis as I cruised toward Connecticut in the cool night. Each of them had a motive. Jeremy's was jealousy, even though I had to admit he didn't seem the type. Cynthia had had money and emotion invested in Augie, and her instability made her a wild-card factor. Jeremy's motive was the soundest.

Davis was innocent of juicing the ball, yet because of Augie he'd been drummed out of baseball. Then there was the not-so-small matter of where had Davis' gun come from? Davis had said he never knew it was missing. Everything pointed back to Jefferson Davis.

If it was a setup, where had the cops been? How did Augie get his gun? Who had the meanest temper and was most likely to lash out in anger?

And yet little edges of doubt nagged at me. I remembered when Davis had hit me with a pitch in the minors. He'd never denied that he'd done it on purpose. Did that count for something? Probably not. Then why in hell did I have this feeling in my gut that the big guy was telling the truth? Maybe I was hanging around Arthur too much.

It was still a couple of hours till sunrise when I pulled into the parking lot of the Manchester Police Department.

I went through the doors and noticed that there was a skeleton crew on duty. A man I hadn't seen before sat with the headphones reading a magazine as he monitored the police band. One of the four cubicles was closed. I walked past the STATE YOUR BUSINESS desk and tapped the guy with the headphones on the shoulder.

He looked up surprised for a second and then he pulled off the headphones. "Something I can do for you, sir?"

"I'm looking for the sheriff," I told him.

"Sheriff Bradford won't be on until later. Say, you're that New York fellow, right? Uhh . . . Redman?"

"Resnick."

"Yes, Resnick. The sheriff's been trying to get you for a couple of hours. He's been working double and triple shifts trying to get a handle on this Casillo business."

"I wasn't home."

"Why don't you have a seat and I'll call him for you. He might still be in his car, he just left about a quarter of an hour ago. He wanted to talk to you real bad."

I saw him put a call through to the sheriff's car. Then I heard a cackling response that sounded like gibberish to me. The communications man understood it perfectly.

"Sheriff says to sit tight. He'll be right back."

I killed some time reading a *Newsweek*, and then took a brief walk around the station house. I thought about whether I would like to finish up my career in law enforcement by becoming a sheriff or a police chief in some small rural town. Too quiet, was my final verdict. I'd be bored to death.

When Bradford strode through the doors, the man in

the communications gear sat on his magazine and was all business.

Bradford nodded to me and then walked over to the fellow with the earphones. "You hear anything from Jesse on the fire at Krane's place?"

"No, sir. He said he was going to check into it and he hasn't called back yet."

"Okay, keep on his tail. A night like this for that boy is tailor-made for cooping. Resnick, you want to come into my office, please?"

I followed Bradford. "I thought cooping was a big-city phenomenon," I said.

"Hell, I got some boys who could show you a thing or two. They've developed it into an art. Trouble is I know it, but I can't seem to catch them at it."

Cooping referred to the practice of cops on patrol pulling off in an isolated spot and sleeping.

"You make them fill out logbooks?"

"Sure, but they can put down anything. As long as I can't verify it, they're clear. I've got two cars, plus my own unmarked vehicle. We're stretched thin sometimes."

That was the cry of every lawman who ever lived, I thought.

"Your man says you've been trying to get in touch with me," I said.

"Yeah."

Bradford made sure the door was closed all the way.

"I owe you an apology for the foul-up this afternoon. I had no idea the guy I deputized had a brother involved in news reporting."

I waved off his explanation. "You covered that on the phone. It happens sometimes. I've had a few like that myself."

"Yeah—well, that's nice of you, to let me off the hook, but the fact of it is that if it were the other way around, I'd be hotter than them Mexican peppers. Anyway, that's not what I wanted to talk to you about."

"Okay—shoot."

Bradford brushed his hand nervously over his "standing at attention" gray hair. He was figuring out the best way to phrase something that was difficult for him.

"Y'see, Slots—that screw-up this afternoon, well—things like that aren't supposed to happen. I guess what I'm feeling is . . ."

He bought himself time by patting his uniform pocket and pulling out a pack of Carletons. He offered one to me, but I shook him down. He lit up and seemed to get courage.

"I think I'm over my head on this case, Slots. Now, you've got to understand that I got jurisdiction here, and I got the okay with the Attorney General to crack it on my own, but shit . . . they put a goddamned microscope on me and I'm getting spooked. That's the whole of it."

"There's been more than a few folks in your position that have felt the same way when a big case came up. If it's any consolation, I've felt it."

I thought about Morris Ackerman and his pipe, blowing Sail tobacco in my face and swearing that if the case wasn't cracked in a day, I'd be pounding a beat in Bensonhurst.

"I'll level with you. I'm scared to death I'll screw up."

"You can pass it on to the State Police," I offered.

"Then the whole world will know I'm chicken shit. I've been here for fifteen years. I've done a lot of good for this town and I've stepped on a few toes along the way. There's some folks who'd like to see me go down."

"Why tell me?"

"I need your help. I need a partner on this thing."

"A silent partner, I suppose."

"I'd make it up to you," he said seriously.

"I don't need to make a name for myself, Bradford,

so I'd be willing to work with you. But there's a condition."

"Name it."

"You do what I say, and don't ask me any questions."

He thought about it. I liked that. If he'd agreed too quickly, it wouldn't have meant much.

He stuck out his hand. "Deal," he said.

We shook on it.

"How long have you kept those logbooks for your staff?"

"We've always had logbooks."

"I want to see the logs of the men from three years ago on the night of December seventh."

He was about to ask why, then he remembered our agreement.

He pressed an intercom on the desk and asked for the books I wanted to be brought into the office. We waited, and Bradford was starting to get impatient. He punched the button on the intercom just as the door opened. A uniformed man placed four books on the desk.

I handed two of the officers' notebooks to Bradford and I took the other two.

"Check the notations for the evening of December seventh. I'm looking to see if someone called in a complaint at the Casillo house. That was the night he was murdered."

Bradford nodded.

I had the notebook of an Officer Burke and an Officer Pike. Bradford had Jessup and Kordel.

It was in Burke's book. The notation was a report of a prowler at the home of Casillo. There was no mention of who had called it in. The report was flashed over the radio at 6:50 P.M. and the next notation was at 7:35 P.M. "Grounds secured, no prowler evident."

"What kind of response time do you have with your patrol cars?" I asked Bradford.

"We can make anyplace in the sector in ten minutes, fifteen tops."

I showed him the forty-five minutes that had elapsed between call and action as written in Burke's book.

Bradford looked puzzled. "I don't get it," he said. "Steve Burke shared a car with Jerry Kordel. Let me check Kordel's book. He's not with us on the force anymore. He had a minor heart attack and retired. Let's see. Okay, here it is. Yeah, now I got it."

"What's it say?"

"Kordel got a call at six fifty-five to investigate a break-in in progress at the pharmacy on the other side of town. They had to check that out first. We usually don't give priority to anonymous tips. See, he's got a notation that the alarm got screwed up by the storm. Yeah, now I remember, we were running around like chickens after that big storm. I remember we called it our Pearl Harbor storm."

"The storm was on the seventh?"

"It started on the sixth, it was a real howler. We had telephone lines knocked down and sporadic power failures. That screwed up a lot of alarm systems. They're supposed to have a battery backup, but if the battery is low, the cutoff in power trips the alarm. We were running all over town. At first we thought there was a bunch of ghosts driving us nuts."

"I want a list of the houses that were blacked out on the sixth and seventh. Can you get that for me?"

"That shouldn't be a problem," Bradford said. "We use Connecticut Light and Power and they got it all on the computer. I'll wait until morning. They open around nine."

"Get someone to look it up now, if you can. Get them out of bed. It's important!"

"If that's what you need, Slots. You want a list of the places where the storm knocked out electric power?"

"Forget the commercial places. I just want residences in the town of Manchester. What time the power went off . . . and when the power went back on."

"For the seventh, right?"

"Sixth and seventh," I told him.

Bradford nodded and made a few calls. "It'll be on my desk in a couple of hours," he said. "I can't push them any faster than that."

Bradford had a water cooler behind his desk. There were two spigots, a red and a blue. He pulled a couple of cups from a desk drawer and a jar of instant coffee.

"I can give you instant coffee or tea," he told me.

"I'll take the coffee, black, no sugar."

He poured the hot water into both of the cups and stirred in the brown granules. I drank mine hoping the caffeine would chase away the fatigue I was beginning to feel.

"What can you tell me about the Marshes?" I asked.

He took a sip from his cup before he spoke. Bradford was very deliberate in everything he did. He didn't offer an opinion until he'd thought it out first in his head. Maybe that's how he'd stayed sheriff for fifteen years, watching all his p's and q's. It made for a good politician, but it must be maddening for his wife.

"You know the old saw about opposites attracting? Well, they must have had those two in mind. She's like a wild untamed mustang, always kicking up her heels and stretching the rules to the limit, maybe over the limit. He's a walking ice cube, or maybe a human computer would be a better description. A lot of folks figured she married him for his money, and Slots, he's got money he ain't never folded yet. The fact of it is, though, that she's an heiress with plenty of scratch herself."

"Did you ever have any run-ins with them?"

"First of all, Slots, you got to know that Jeremy Marsh donates a lot of money to this town, in addition to the taxes that he pays, which are considerable. We've got one of the finest gyms in the state in our high

194

school; Marsh contributed that. We got a brand-new police cruiser, that came from Jeremy. He's a good friend of the Mayor. He puts his money up front in our political campaigns and he wields a lot of influence around here."

"So you're saying that he knows how to win friends and influence people."

"Well," he took another swallow of coffee as he composed his thoughts, "let's say a lot of the things Cynthia has done over the years might have carried a lot more weight if Jeremy wasn't around with his checkbook to lighten the load."

"You've got an example?"

"There was an incident here a couple of weeks ago. Cynthia stopped off in town to do a little shopping. Mr. Harris, he's an elderly gent with eyesight problems who really shouldn't be driving but somehow he passes all the state license exams, backs his car up in the lot and smacks into Cynthia's. Well, he leaves this little dent and a little scrape. She comes out and sees it and she goes berserk. She pulls a bat from her trunk and smashes every one of Harris' windows and batters his car all over. Now, this is all happening with Harris sitting behind the wheel and holding his hands over his head in mortal fear. Then Cynthia climbs into her car and calmly drives off."

"What happened? Did Harris press charges?"

"He sure did, but dropped them immediately."

"Why?"

"Well, Jeremy wrote him this nice note of apology, and pinned it to the windshield of a shiny new Cadillac that found its way to Harris' driveway."

"What's her poison? Drugs? Alcohol?"

"Name it, Slots, she's done it all. We've held her on drunk-and-disorderly a few times. I know my guys have stopped her on the road dozens of times. Somehow the Breathalyzer is always broken when they pick her up. They drive her home and Jeremy promises it won't happen again. We once had her blood tested, with Jeremy's permission. She overdosed on something and almost didn't make it. We got back a report that the technician couldn't believe. The lady had enough different kinds of shit in her to kill a team of horses."

"I hear she screws around."

"You got that right. Doesn't make any bones about it. She sees a man she wants and þam, she's in the sack. You've seen her, haven't you, Slots? With a package like that, she's not going to be wanting for takers."

"What's Jeremy's reaction?"

I waited for Bradford to get his story down. It was becoming a pattern that I expected by now.

"Very strange. He must know. Everybody in town and even the neighboring towns knows about Cynthia. He never seems to let it bother him. Like I said, the fellow is the Iceman. Ernie out there, the guy on the radio, has this theory. He says maybe Jeremy gets a kick out of Cynthia's escapades. Like maybe he has her tell him all about what she does with men and he gets off on it."

"What about Cynthia and Augie Casillo?"

"That was the big news around here for a while. Augie had the winters off work, and Jeremy was out of town a lot. They were very open about their affair. It lasted until Theresa got sick. Augie sort of had a bad case of the guilts. See, Theresa was a very religious woman, very quiet, and along comes Cynthia like a tornado and sweeps him up. Augie came back to his senses when Theresa was hospitalized. He was by her side throughout her ordeal. It was like he was making it up to her."

"Could Jeremy have feared that with Theresa dead, Augie would come back and take Cynthia away from him?"

Bradford shook his head. "No way. He had been through this with Cynthia a dozen times already. They have this kind of weird relationship, she and Jeremy.

196

She gets into trouble, he straightens it out, she goes running back to him. She has an affair, he waits until she gets tired of the guy, and then she runs back to him. He's willing to accept anything she does. I can't see him killing Casillo."

I finished my coffee and leaned back in the chair. The picture Bradford had given me about Jeremy and Cynthia confirmed my own feelings about them. I felt a little uncomfortable being another notch on Cynthia's sexual gun.

"Slots, how come you're so interested in the Marshes? What happened to Davis as a suspect?"

"I saw Davis this evening."

"What? Police from three states are looking for him!"

"They won't find him."

I felt I had to share something with Bradford. Our "partnership" couldn't be a one-way road. I told him Jeff's side of the story and watched his reaction.

"It doesn't make sense to me," Bradford said. "Where did the gun come from? Why would he get rid of Augie's body?"

"Here's a better question. Who called in the complaint of a prowler around Augie's house on December seventh?" I asked him.

"I don't know." Bradford shrugged. "Lots of times people don't want to get involved. They call in the squeal and then stay out of it."

"Sheriff, you had this big snowstorm on December sixth that lasted through the seventh. How many people do you know that would be walking around in that storm? How many people would be able to notice or hear a prowler in the wind and snow? And where the hell were they able to find a phone on a country road and report Davis the same minute that he arrived at Augie's house?"

"Damn, Slots, you're right!"

"The way it looks is that Davis was supposed to get

caught by your men standing over the body with his gun, except your patrol car got sidetracked by a burglary in progress."

"Slots, what if it was a suicide and Augie was behind the setup?"

"It's possible, but I would tend to rule it out. I can't see any motive for Casillo to frame Davis. The other way around would make more sense. Also, Casillo had no idea when he'd be back in the States. When Theresa died, he supposedly called Jeremy to ask him to open up his house and start the boiler going. My guess is that he also had the phones shut off."

"So where does that leave us?" he wanted to know. "There goes our number-one suspect."

"Maybe."

"You just said that someone wanted to set Davis up. Now you're saying it could still be Davis?"

"Maybe Davis got here before seven. What if Davis killed Augie, dumped him in the lake, and then called in a report of a prowler long after he was on the road back to Newark? He'd know there'd be a police record of the call, and then he could scream SETUP!"

Bradford mulled that over. I didn't tell him that Jeremy had claimed to be a witness and said that he had seen someone, presumably Davis, carrying Augie to the lake. The key was the time element. If Davis had plotted this out, what time did he arrive? If Jeremy saw him around seven, the chances were that Davis was innocent of Augie's murder, even if he was guilty of gross stupidity. Another thing that was troubling me was Jeremy's claim that he'd heard Augie arguing. Was that just the howling wind? Was Jeremy lying?

"Jesus, Slots, we just seem to be spinning our wheels."

I gave Bradford a smile. "Sometimes it goes that way. I'm going to need a couple of things from you, Sheriff. Do you have a good flashlight?"

"Sure, what else?"

"I'll need a car with a radio. Feel like switching with me for the morning?"

"That little black Porsche your car?"

"It belongs to the finance company, but I can drive it as long as I can come up with the payments once a month."

"Maybe I'll set up along the highway and run down some speeders with it," he kidded. "You want to tell me what you're up to?"

"I think it might be better for you if you didn't know. This way, if things blow up in my face, you're not a party to anything."

"Gotcha. Should I be doing anything in the meantime?"

"Just stick around until I can get that report from Connecticut Light and Power."

"I don't get it . . . but whatever you say."

The sheriff's car was a late-model Ford Fairlane, equipped with a Jensen police radio. I pulled away from the station house and tried a radio check with Ernie in the communications room. He was reading me "five-by-five."

It would still be an hour or so until daybreak. Like most people who spend their time in the city, I was intrigued by the brightness and number of stars in the clear, black country sky. How long had this been going on, and why couldn't we get the stars in New York? There was probably some guy on Park Avenue who had the franchise, and if you wanted to see stars in New York, there was an initial hook-up fee and a monthly charge.

Slot Resnick, resident cynic.

I pulled into the Casillo driveway just as icy-fingered dawn stretched her gossamer tendrils of pink and yellow over the ridge of the eastern sky.

Slots Resnick, resident poet, and getting punchy from lack of sleep.

I used the sheriff's big flashlight to find the boarded window of least resistance. A couple of hard kicks knocked out the slats and gave me a hole big enough to get my body through.

It was a skeleton of a house now; whatever had been of the slightest value long gone, taken by human scavengers. I tried to imagine what it must have looked like. The door led into a small hall that took you into a large sunken living room. I could see a spot for a piano near the stairs leading to the upstairs bedrooms. The living room sofa would be near the far wall, maybe a modular setup around a coffee table.

I stood at the inside of the front door and shone my light toward the direction of the kitchen. You could see the kitchen from the door. If there had been a man sitting at a table with his back to the door, Davis could have seen him—but not in the dark, not at seven in a storm in December. The lights would have had to be on.

I walked into the kitchen as Davis had said he'd done and I imagined the spot where Augie had been supposed to be sitting. Davis had said he nudged him and the umpire slumped forward. He saw the other side of the head shattered by a bullet.

What about blood? Davis hadn't said. Did he wipe up the blood? It would depend on the angle of the bullet. I had seen bullets that had entered a body and exited in such a way that the blood was actually cauterized. A medical examiner had once ruled a person dead of natural causes only to find a clean bullet hole under the victim's hair.

I pictured Davis seeing the body and then, with horror, looking down and seeing his own gun on the floor. Davis panics. He tucks the gun in his waistband, and then carries Augie, fireman style, out the door, remembering to shut the lights and close the door behind him.

Later, when the patrol car would come by, they

would look over the property and find nothing out of the ordinary. The tracks that Jeremy had talked about would have been covered over quickly by the falling snow.

I walked upstairs. Some of the stairs were broken, the banister a rickety affair on its last legs. There were three bedrooms, no furniture, and nothing else of relevance to the case.

Back downstairs, I found the door leading to the basement. It was finished in wood paneling. There was a wall filled with nail holes, possibly the place Augie had kept plaques and baseball mementos.

I walked past the main room to a little nook where the washing machine and dryer must have been kept, and finally the closeted boiler. It was a fairly new Burnham model 4b gas boiler. Starting it would be simple enough. It meant flipping a switch and making sure the automatic water feed was working. Jeremy had claimed Augie had wanted him to heat the house.

I went back upstairs and turned off the flash. It was a bright morning and the sun made me squint as I crawled back out the window I had used to get in. I walked down to the lake, which was about thirty yards from the house.

It would have been a difficult carry for most people, but Davis was an animal. He could carry Augie with ease, and then back again.

I retraced my steps to the sheriff's vehicle and called in. The sheriff's handle written over the top of the radio was Eagle 1.

"This is Mobile Unit one, calling Eagle one, over."

"Hold on, one, Eagle will be right with you."

"Roger."

"Mobile one, this is Eagle one, come in."

"Do you have that information, Eagle?"

"Affirmative," Bradford said.

I looked at the Casillo house number. It was 1714.

"What were hours of closing for one-seven-one-four?"

There was a brief pause and then Bradford's voice again. "Casillo residence, Mobile one?"

"Affirmative."

"Okay, power off as of twelve-six two P.M. through twelve-seven four P.M. Do you copy?"

"December 6, two P.M. through December 7, four P.M."

"That's a Roger."

"Check the Marsh estate. It must be one-seven-one-six."

"Affirmative. No interruption of power. They must be hooked to a separate feed line."

"Okay, I copy. Over and out."

The lights in the Casillo house had been on when Davis arrived. That part of his story checked. Jeremy had said that he put on Augie's boiler after a call on the sixth. The call had come in during the late afternoon hours. That meant that Jeremy had had to work in the dark.

I walked the mile or so distance between the two houses. Even at a quick pace, it would have to taken ten minutes. There were no roadside phones.

• • • • • • • • • • • • • • • •

17

The Marsh concrete bunker looked even more impressive in the morning. It was as if the forest had been scooped up in one spot and replaced by the massive gray structure.

I walked around to the door and rang the bell. I didn't expect anyone to be up, it was just half past six, so I kept my finger on the bell and tried to hum "Jingle Bells" to myself in time to the ringing.

The housekeeper came to the door in a bathrobe. I could tell she recognized me. "Do you know what time it is?" she asked.

"Time to let me in and wake up Monsieur and Madame. Let them get dressed and meet me in the living room."

"I'll do no such thing!" she said, crossing her hands across her chest.

"Then I'm going to have to throw rocks at their window until they wake up, and then they're going to be mad at you. This is official police business, and if you don't move, I'm going to ask the sheriff to take you into jail and hold you as an accessory."

She was thinking it over as I bent down and picked up a good-sized rock.

"All right!"

She opened the door and let me in.

"You'll have to wait in the living room while I see if they want to see you. I hope they don't bite my head off for waking them."

I followed her lead and took a seat in the beautiful living room.

Jeremy Marsh was the first one down. Betty was close on his heels.

"Resnick! It's an ungodly hour," he said in that foppish way of his.

"Sorry, but I'm on a tight schedule. Where's the lovely Mrs. Marsh?"

"She's still sleeping. She didn't get in till very late last night. I'd rather not wake her."

"Wake her! Either Betty does it, or it'll be Sheriff Bradford!"

Jeremy's eyes narrowed. He turned to Betty and nodded. He was wearing a purple satin robe over a pair of monogrammed blue pajamas, and brown open-toe bedroom slippers.

"You had better come up with a good reason for this, Resnick. I have friends in New York who will help me if I need a favor. Your license has to be renewed every year, doesn't it?"

"Don't worry about my license," I told him offhandedly. "You've got other things to worry about."

If I thought that would rattle him, I was wrong. Marsh simply sighed, folded his hands in his lap and waited.

Cynthia arrived a few moments later. She wore a robe that matched Jeremy's, and although her eyes seemed sunken in and her hair was askew, she was still lovely.

"What time is it?" she asked hoarsely.

"It's six-thirty, my dear. Mr. Resnick has something to talk to us about. It's very mysterious," he said.

"Are you crazy?" she asked, flopping down next to her husband. She leaned her head back and closed her eyes.

"Why didn't you tell me it was you who called the police to report a prowler?"

"What makes you think I did?" he said with a slight hint of amusement.

"No one else was out in the storm, and if they were, you would have seen them."

"I suppose I should have mentioned it to you, Mr. Resnick, but as I said before, I'm not one to get involved. I felt it was my civic duty, however, to report what I heard. I don't think I was required to give my name, and I didn't break any law by not mentioning it to you, did I?"

"The police record shows the call coming in at six-fifty on the seventh. Davis told me he didn't arrive at the house until seven. Would you explain to me how it was possible for you to report a prowler ten minutes before Davis got there?"

"Yes, that's quite obvious, isn't it? Davis must have made a mistake, or he's lying. He must have gotten to Augie's earlier. I saw what I told you, and drove back to my home and called the police."

"Amazing how Davis didn't hear your car's motor."

"The wind was howling."

"But you could hear two men shouting at each other through a closed door?"

"Yes—yes, I could," Jeremy said stonily.

"You went to Casillo's house the evening before he died."

"Yes. I told you he asked me to put on his furnace."

"Did you notice anything strange?"

"No, why should I?"

"Did you notice that the lights weren't working?"

"I don't recall."

"Let me refresh your memory," I said. "The storm caused a blackout in some of Manchester's houses. Not

205

yours, Jeremy, but Augie's house was without power during the time you say you went over there."

"Yes, you're right. I believe I took a flashlight with me. Yes, I had a light that I used. I let myself downstairs and put on the furnace. As a matter of fact, Jack Morris was out plowing the roads and he saw me leaving Augie's house."

"Where's Augie's money?"

"I suppose he spent it."

"That's a lot of money to spend."

"For you, perhaps." Jeremy shrugged.

"You cleared three million dollars on that little scam. The government is going to be very interested in seeing what became of it."

"What are you getting at, Mr. Resnick, other than wasting my time?"

"I think you killed Augie. I think Augie called you from Mexico and he threatened to tell Davis that he framed him with the Vaseline in the glove. He wanted his share of the money you won. I think you were holding out on him."

"That's an interesting theory, Resnick, but you're wrong. It was my wife's scheme, and she and Casillo split the money they made."

"We'll find that out, won't we? We're going to find out a lot of things about the respectable Mr. Jeremy Marsh. You and Augie framed Davis with that Vaseline scam, and then you killed Augie to keep him quiet."

"You'll have to prove that."

"The publicity would ruin you, though, Jeremy," Cynthia said.

I thought she had been sleeping. Her eyes were closed, and they stayed closed.

"Shut up, Cynthia!" Jeremy told her.

"No, I can't let them try to pin this on you."

It was working out the way I had hoped it would.

"I said, *shut up!*" It was the closest I'd seen of Marsh losing his cool.

206

"Jeremy, it doesn't matter. If it's over—well, I'm tired of living with it anyway. I killed Augie, Slots."

"You fool. You stupid fool!" Jeremy said softly.

"My husband has been covering up for me too long, Slots. I don't want him to be ruined because of me. Whatever happens to me doesn't matter. Jeremy had nothing to do with the scam either. It was all me and Augie. I did it for laughs. I did it to see if I could get away with it."

"Why did you kill Augie?"

"I don't know. He must have told me he was leaving me. He must have felt guilty after Theresa died. I don't know."

"What do you mean, 'you don't know'?" I questioned.

"My wife has blackouts, Mr. Resnick. Years ago she had been drinking quite heavily and the blackouts were quite frequent."

"You're telling me that she killed Augie during one of these blackouts?"

"That's what happened, Slots," Cynthia insisted. "Jeremy told me the truth two days ago."

"Where did you get Davis' gun?" I asked her.

"That was Augie's idea. Augie knew players on Davis' team. They all said how dangerous it was for a hothead like Jefferson Davis to have a gun. Augie got cold feet. He was afraid that Davis might try to go after him. I suggested he steal the gun."

"How?"

"Augie waited until he and his crew were assigned to work a series with Davis' team. The league often booked the umpires in the same hotel as the players. Augie got himself invited to a poker game that the coaches and some of the sportswriters took part in when they were on the road. Augie was able to get a passkey and take the gun from Davis' room."

"Just like that," I said sarcastically.

"Look. The players have a one-o'clock curfew when

they have a game the next day. The team always assigns a coach to go around and do a bed check. Augie knew the coach who had the passkey. He borrowed it from him by saying he'd forgotten his own key and he had to go to his room to bring some fresh money into the game. The coach handed Augie the passkey without giving it a second thought. Augie went up to Davis' room and found the gun in a travel bag. He took it, and then went back down to the game and returned the key. Davis probably never knew the gun was gone, and if he did, he probably figured it was a prank, because all the guys on the team were nervous about that wild man carrying a gun."

"How did you get the gun?" I asked her.

"I don't know. All I remember was Jeremy slapping me awake. The gun was in my hand and Augie was dead."

"I did hear arguing, Mr. Resnick. It was Cynthia and Augie arguing. I had offered Augie an additional million dollars if he'd leave Cynthia for good. They were arguing because Augie had decided to take my offer."

"Why did Augie call Davis?" I asked.

"He wanted to straighten things out with Davis. He was going to offer him some money. He had the gun ready in case Davis wouldn't go for the peace offering and got violent."

"I must have been so angry I went for the gun and shot him," Cynthia said tearfully.

"So Jeremy decided to clean up his wife's mess once again," I said. "You wiped off the prints and put the gun near Augie on the floor. Your first defense was to have people think Augie killed himself. Then you thought about it and decided it might look even better if Davis was caught with the gun in his hand. So you brought Cynthia back home, and called the sheriff's office with the anonymous tip.

"Unfortunately for you, the cops were on another errand and got there too late to catch Jefferson. You were hanging around in hiding waiting for them to arrive. You couldn't know that Jefferson would dump the body in the lake. When the police didn't arrive in time, it made no difference to you. Jefferson had done the work for you, and if nobody ever found Augie, so much the better.

"Then I come around a few years later asking about Augie and you get worried that I might stumble onto something. You had Mr. Faine tail me with the idea of rubbing me out."

"I'd do anything to protect my wife!" he said defiantly.

"Sure you would. But what you really mean is that you'd do anything to protect yourself, even put your wife in prison."

"What are you talking about?" Cynthia said.

"You're insane!" Marsh snapped.

"Don't you see, Cynthia? Jeremy built up a wall of defense to protect himself. First he made Augie's death look like a suicide. Then he decided to hedge his bet by implicating Davis. Then he tried to take me out of the picture by bringing in a hit man. Now, with his back against the wall, he's playing his trump card . . . *you.*"

"It's not true! I've always helped Cynthia get out of trouble."

"Maybe, but this little game of hers was too dangerous. This one involved bookmakers connected with the Mafia, and the feds, and it was too hot for you to let continue."

"Are you saying I didn't kill Augie?" Cynthia said, staring at her husband.

"Don't listen to him!" Marsh told her.

"Here's the way it happened, Cynthia. Augie called and said he was going to make a clean breast of things. Theresa had made him promise to straighten up his life. That's the only reason I can see for him to call Davis. After all, his wife had just died. Why would the first two calls he makes go to Davis and Jeremy?"

"He wanted me to heat up his house. He was going to get some papers and leave town," Jeremy insisted.

"He was going to tell Davis what really happened. He called you to tell you what he was going to do, Cynthia. Jeremy intercepted the call and found out what his plans were. Either you were drunk, or he got you drunk enough to pass out. He took you with him to Casillo's house, and argued with Augie while you slept.

"He hadn't come over the day before to put on the furnace. He'd spent that time looking for Davis' gun, which you or Casillo must have told him about. He only made up the furnace story because the man on the snowplow saw him walk out of the house and Jeremy knew that someday that might come out."

"Ridiculous!" Jeremy was yelling, the suave businessman gone. "I heated up Augie's house. That's what he asked me to do!"

"When Jeremy couldn't shake Augie's decision to spill the whole story to Davis, he shot him. Then he woke you up and put the gun in your hand."

"Jeremy! Did you? *Did you?*"

"Don't let him break us up, Cynthia. We're a team. He's lying. I've always looked out for you."

"I need a drink," Cynthia said.

I was too tired and my reactions too slow.

When she turned from the bar she had a pistol in her hand. "I want to know the truth, Jeremy," she said in a dull voice.

"I've told you the truth! He's the one that's putting the doubt in your mind."

"He could take anything you did, Cynthia, but he couldn't take the idea of losing his business and being ruined. He saw a chance to crawl out. It's too bad he decided to use you as his last resort."

"Jeremy, if you could do that to me, then—then I have nothing! I've always depended on you."

"You can still depend on me. Just give me the gun."

"I felt so bad when you told me that I killed Augie."

"I know—I know. Point the gun at Resnick and squeeze the trigger. We can be together again. Nothing will come between us. Kill Resnick, Cynthia. You've got to kill Resnick."

"Do you swear you didn't use me?"

"I swear. Give me the gun, Cynthia. If you won't use it, I will. We'll say we heard a burglar. We'll kill him and our problems will be over."

Cynthia was unsteady on her feet. She seemed to wobble and have trouble focusing. Jeremy saw it and started to walk toward her.

"Get back!" she warned him.

"You took too many pills this morning. Give me the gun," he said.

"Cynthia," I told her, "think about what he said. He told you that he didn't go to Augie's house to look for the gun. He told you he went to light the furnace."

"That's true," Jeremy said.

"But he couldn't light the furnace. The furnace won't go on without electric power."

"It's a gas furnace, Cynthia, not electric," Jeremy said.

"The starter is electric," I told her. "He couldn't start the furnace if the pilot needed an electric starter!"

Cynthia stared at Jeremy. "He's right. I remember once when a circuit breaker was tripped, the furnace wouldn't go on. You lied!!"

"Cynthia, please . . . I . . . I . . . know what's best for you. I always have!"

Cynthia looked at him and shook her head. "There is no best for me, Jeremy. There isn't anything. I just want the pain to stop." She sighed, placed the gun in her mouth and fired.

"*Cynthia, NO-O-O-O-O-O!*" Jeremy screamed and ran toward her.

He cradled her in his arms. I had my .38 ready in case he went for the gun, but he didn't. He held her in his arms.

And Jeremy "the Iceman" Marsh cried.

· · · · · · · · · · · · · · · · ·

18

For people like me who measure the year in months till spring training, and then days till opening day, this was the best of times.

I sat in the stands, my eyes closed, letting the first real warm sun of spring wash over my upturned face. There was the smell of freshly mowed grass and the steady tattoo of baseballs batted into outstretched gloves. There was something ageless in the games of pepper and the tracking down of fungoes, the long fly balls coaches always managed to hit just out of your reach. There were the sounds of young men, needling each other, cheering each other, and striving to meet the challenge of a curve ball or a rising line drive.

With my eyes closed, I was out there with them. Slots Resnick, gliding over the infield and practicing the pivot on the double play.

I could hear all the familiar sounds and remember what it was like when I played a million years ago and hit a home run off Jefferson "Nightmare" Davis.

I opened my eyes and looked down on the field. A

generation of new players were taking their turns in the April sunshine.

Harry Quinn handed me a hot dog, and Theda poured some cold beer into my glass from a thermos she had brought with her.

Theda was smiling and enjoying herself. She seemed to have taken off years, she was no longer the frightened, drawn woman I had met a few short months ago.

Arthur was on the mound. He looked in for a sign and threw the first pitch right by the swinging batter.

Theda's friend, a man named Thomas, applauded the pitch. "Hey, that boy of yours can throw!" he said in admiration.

The next pitch was a curve that the hitter flailed at, missing by at least a foot.

"Take a look over there," Harry said, pointing a bony finger at the man standing near the center-field gate.

"Jefferson?"

"Yeah, he comes to every game," Harry said. "Then he takes Arthur out for dinner and they talk about how to pitch."

A few days after Marsh was arrested, Jefferson had come into my office. It was unexpected, and I wondered what he wanted.

"I . . . I guess I got to say thanks."

"Forget it," I told him. "I'm glad you're finally getting a fair shake."

He nodded. "I owe you, Resnick," he said softly.

"If you feel that way, do something for me."

"Yeah? What is it you want?"

"Just give the kid a little something. It doesn't have to be much, Jefferson, just a little something."

He nodded. "He's some kind of kid, ain't he?"

"Some kind of kid," I agreed.

The next two pitches were out of the strike zone. The hitter dug in at the plate. He was setting himself up for a good pitch. Arthur took his sign and blasted a fastball high and inside, making the batter fall back on his duff.

214

I thought I saw Arthur turn around and look toward center where the man nodded his head in approval. I could have told the kid at the plate what to expect. I remembered the sequence of pitches from another time, and from a bigger version of the strapping young pitcher on the mound now.

I watched as the slow curve ball made the batter duck out of the way and then arc like a rainbow over the heart of the plate.

"Strike three!" the umpire hollered.

From center field the big man was clapping his hands. "That's my boy!" he yelled, his voice carrying to the mound, where Arthur's face broke into a beaming smile.

I would have to take Paul Bradford up on his offer to take me fishing. He wanted me to go out on a two-day camping trip. It might be nice to get a look at the stars again, I thought.

I was thinking less these days about the beautiful rich girl who seemed to have it all . . . but who had to kill herself to stop the pain.

Soon that memory would fade too, and all that would remain would be the stars, the sun, and an aging infielder still trying to make the pivot on a hot smash to short.